THE DEVIL IN THE MAIL

Stories

Gbanabom Hallowell

Sierra Leonean Writers Series (SLWS)

The Devil in the Mail

Copyright © 2022 by Gbanabom Hallowell

ISBN: 979-88458-55-07-7

This is a work of fiction. Except in a few obvious instances, names, places, institutions and incidents are either products of the author's imagination or have been used fictitiously. Any resemblance to actual events, places, or persons alive or dead is purely coincidental

Sierra Leonean Writers Series (SLWS)
Warima/Freetown/Accra
120 Kissy Road, Freetown, Sierra Leone
Publisher: Prof. Osman Sankoh (Mallam O.)
publisher@sl-writers-series.org
www.sl-writers-series.org

CONTENTS

LETTER TO FREETOWN

Ten thousand children emerged naked from the dark woods of the peninsula. They ran up the mountain, climbing higher and higher toward the summit. The older ones among them wore calicos around their waists, and the younger ones had shaved their heads to the skin. Barefooted, breathing heavily, they ran up the black animal rock, which a conquistador had christened Kaibara five hundred years ago, because it reminded him of a land with a hard surface of bad soil and high vexatious mountains.

The children's sweltering bodies merged with the rock. The sun roasted their blood, and their skins dripped with sweat. Another group of ten thousand children, with very much the same appearance, but with guns taller than they were and ammo belts tangled across their chests, chased after the first ten thousand.

Suddenly, I saw myself in the narrow gap between the two groups. The pursued group seized me by the right hand and cried, "Help us!" The other group, pulling me by the left hand shouted, "Give way!"

They began to tear me apart.

The dream soaked me from head to toe.

At once a sore opened in my heart. I couldn't stop sweating. I felt like buckets of tears streamed down my face, and the devil's red moon roamed through my lungs, igniting a pain deep inside me.

My exile was already an old hag dreaming of a coffin full of bones every night and with the new dream, I decided it was time to go home across the threatening seas to my native land and cry over my polychromatic pain.

It was time to come out of exile! My dream prompted a knock, one hundred doors behind me.

In the waking world, I attempted to wade gently through the familiar waters of social intercourse at the height of a hurricane season, trying to reconnect with the world.

A voice told me to begin a journey along the nostalgic route like men of letters. But how was I to begin a letter, for instance, to a woman who had lo-ng forgotten me?

How was I to avoid sounding romantic to an old lover when addressing the political affair of the past of my country? Besides, in my exile, the past, the present, and the future had already formed in me something dirty that came from the bowels of the muddy pigs in my forgotten republic.

I remembered reading a book talking about the past being a foreign country. What if that past was trapped in the teeth of a hungry alligator?

What if the embers of convoluted events lingered to brighten the mortal cavern of night?

What if the waters of the banked rivers rushed into rude tributaries and washed over the republic so recently reclaimed, precocious although still not fully formed? What if the past was the consequence of a rabid interaction that left the independence emitting unending pus that stank for a while and then dried up?

The thought of a republic writhing like someone raped by a devil bigger than that of any mortal took away all pretext of innocent gentility.

The lugubrious image of Miss Havisham, with her bedraggled wedding dress, stepped out of Charles Dickens' *Great Expectations* and seemed to look out at me from the blank page on which I attempted to set down words to my former mistress, M'balu, who had been renamed Vanessa (a name I had found romantic) by her Krio guardians in the early '50s.

It was fashionable then for natives to be christened with European names. This practice appeared to hang a tag around the necks of black monkeys just rescued from the thick and impenetrable ignorance of the African jungles. European names indicated that their owners had been saved by droplets of water sprinkled on their heads or by having been dipped in the open mouth of bedeviled streams in the full view of a million unfortunate others still buried in the foam of darkness. However, compelled by her traditional roots and the adult shame of her teenage wetness, Vanessa had since reclaimed her native name.

M'balu, my very own Miss Havisham, carried a wound which Victorian England required Dickens to blur in his character. It bled onto the thick layer of dust on her, such as on the wedding dress of colonial promise.

The colonial legacies of makeshift structures and narrow streets in my beloved republic characterized the lugubrious nature of the immediate post-colonial African extracted from a jungle and set to hang on the backdoor of a new civilization continually blown by the harsh wind of European culture.

On the white sheet before me, I wanted to write about the incongruous graffiti of Miss Havisham's dual selves: each self constantly detaching from the other like two spent dogs in post-coital exhaustion. Each, a shadow of the other, yet very much an independent entity.

Alienated from my wife and daughter, from both marriage and fatherhood, I experienced the hunger of loneliness. In the beginning, it seemed as if my loneliness flowed through me like a breath of freedom before returning from across mirroring streams to take possession of me in my sleep.

I had never known a word or a phrase, capable of describing this kind of hunger. However, because this hunger brought with it a disturbing physical aspect, like the contractions of a prolonged past, I believed it was real.

In reason, I agreed with my instinct that I must reconnect with my country, Kaibara, if I were ever to know relief from this hunger. With my wife and daughter gone out of my life, I had no friends to hang out with in New York City. Reconnecting with the motherland, therefore, promised nostalgic rejuvenation. Already, vivid African images surged in my head: the noise of an African family cooking the daily meal, the clash of mortar and pestle in the practiced hands of little maids, a crawling man-eating python, and the opportunity of the community man-child to display to the applause of spectators his bravery in wrestling the snake with its vicious teeth.

I still hadn't forgotten the news of the mysterious death of my friend, Archibald in RoMarong City. He had spent his last days in incarceration, living and dying by his conscience. As I considered him, my mind recalled the gleaming beige of the blood-starved republic, but I was soon catapulted into a sense of the present and the future. Thus, I felt the need to be cautious in composing my letter to M'balu.

My dear M'balu, accept my apology for the long silence between us.

I paused to examine what I had written. Something about it seemed inappropriate. To open with an apology, I thought, might create a psychic tension between M'balu and me, and I didn't want to admit guilt to her for anything I didn't consider wrong on my part. I also convinced myself that with the burden of the war still heavy on her mind, the sense of presenting myself to her as a victim might vaguely link me, in her mind, to Kaibara's butchers, whose spiritual destruction would undoubtedly remain a deep-seated agony to her.

My dear M'balu, I always remember you in my prayers. God knows that a fine person like you has no reason to be locked up in the mess our country has been thrown into.

Again, I felt uneasy about what I had written, but I lacked the will to work on my wording. The ineluctable power of the words reverberated in me. I was impressed that the words sharply and directly expressed my feelings for both Kaibara and M'balu. Though I was not so sure that God knew M'balu anymore as a fine person, I was equally unsure if some wicked god had thrown Kaibara into the war that now devastated it.

I felt that M'balu should have repudiated the choice of her parents just as I felt that Kaibara should have known better than to haul itself into the mess into which it was now sinking.

In writing a letter to an estranged but long-standing acquaintance such as M'balu, I would do well to recall some of the striking moments we had spent together. Looking up from the paper, I let my gaze fall upon the Venetian blinds in front of me where M'balu was fading in as a newly lighted candle. As I stared at them, I saw in my mind the washed garment dragged from under bodies in a battlefield, imprinted with the many images of *my* Miss Havisham as she turned from an aborted wedding. Pale white, hung as though dripping the blood of ten thousand wars.

M'balu quickly vanished behind the Venetian slats into unseen moments. I persuaded myself to believe that if I lifted those blinds and allowed my perception a free rein, I would not only wash my mind of battlements, but also, I would regain a handful of memorable events of our past together.

Walking toward the window, I recited her name. I must have said it ten times before reaching the blinds. "M'balu" conveyed granite warmth whereas he "Vanessa" counterpart simply mesmerized. However, for the sake of the letter I set myself to write, I needed to stay hard and dry.

Beyond my window, New York City's river flowed before me like the sagacious RoMarong City River on the edge of my beloved Kaibara. The RoMarong City River ran into the Atlantic Ocean where the Creek broke its neck and spread below the city, giving rise to my Nova Scotian, dark Anglo-Saxon Krio ancestry.

At once I heard the rolling of the parched waves and imagined them exploding against the pubescent legs of M'balu. She was there, surrendering her body to the golden sand upon which she curled in serpentine bliss, her hands held high above the water in the salubrious wind, beckoning me to join her in defying the *munkle,* a Themne word she had taught me. It jumped into my head, liberated from its attendant meaning. Yet as I fabricated a role for *munkle*, I heard M'balu whispering to me from the alcoves of a raw feminine independence that *munkle* stood for the sea waves. At that moment, the brilliant color of one memorable moment rushed to mind.

"It's not fair, Desmond! It's not fair!" M'balu had shouted to me across Lumley Beach, her grief diluting the impassioned brutality of the waves.

I shouted back without raising my head, "Almost finished, darling. The paper is almost through, writing itself!"

"How can you do that to me? Did I come here to watch you bow over political papers? You are spoiling the fun. Even the sea takes notice of your quaint behavior! Must I—"

"Almost there, darling," I insisted. "At the tail end of it, the very tail end," I paused for a moment and closed the gap between us. "I'm sure you want to see me make a good impression tomorrow, don't you?"

She emerged before me like a serpent, her nudity inspiring a liquid attraction. My eyes followed the water rivulets that trickled down her thighs. Lost in her legend, I failed to realize she had seized the papers I was working on and had neatly tossed them inside one of the bags. Then she dove headlong into the water, beckoning me to follow. When she broke the surface, she discovered me standing and mapping out her body's complex shape. We both plunged, she in my arms and me wrapped between her legs.

We resurfaced and achieved a watery balance.

"You mean so much to me," I said.

She understood what I meant.

Her stare came upon me as bright as oil on Harmattan skin. I inhaled its fire.

"Why then wouldn't you allow yourself to mean the same to me at this moment? My time with you is limited. Soon you'll be shackled by the watchful eyes of your Krio girl," she said, placing her palms against the surface of the water as she hung her head.

I quickly realized how hard it was for her to open her heart, but I wanted to tease her. How well she had practiced her speech, especially considering how reserved she had always been about letting me into her mind. I knew that this was her moment, and the best I could do was not to discourage her while her eyes poured *marro* (as she called oil in her language).

I thrust a leg between hers and with one hand pulled her toward me, allowing for the water to lap between us. Making love in the middle of a torrent was not something I dared, but I pulled off a clever stunt. I allowed the gushing water to overturn me. I brought my head to brush against her hair as we let the jealous waves wash us ashore.

"I know I have to watch you speak tomorrow at the rally, but I'll not be as close to you as I'm right now or as I would like to be then. Allow me the pleasure of recalling this moment while you growl into that microphone of yours." M'balu had barely finished speaking when she dragged me again into the water, both of us laughing at the exuberant earnestness of her words.

INVADING FREETOWN

Cyberspace is the funhouse mirror of our society"
Bruce Sterling

"I only have three minutes left, and I have to go."

The response to her typescript on the computer screen was delayed for thirty seconds before it came popping up. All the while Maneta's index finger unconsciously tapped the edge of the keyboard.

"What? Why? Just when it was beginning to get interesting!"

"I have to go! I only paid for thirty minutes, and you and I only became friends five minutes ago; since that time, you have not said anything. You don't even have your picture on your wall. How do I know you are real?"

"Why don't we start from there?"

"No time for that right now. I am in a public cafe and my time is up." Her fingers typed the last sentence faster than ever. She pounded her own keys more noisily than the other keyboards in the room.

"Nor broke am oh!"
She refused to be intimidated by that interference.

"Sign back in and..."
The screen blanked out. In three seconds, it turned sky blue and a small window appeared with the command for her to sign in. She sat back, heaved a big sigh and stared at the screen. She felt a hand on her shoulder. She didn't show any emotion, because she knew what the hand on her shoulder signified.

"Alright, alright, I know, I know, you rogues," she panted.

"You know, and you always have to wait for me to inform you that someone else is waiting to use the computer, or for the screen to go blank on you?"

"Don't shout at me, you must appreciate the fact that I am a regular customer at your cafe."

"Then you must know better than to always pay for thirty minutes if you want to stay for a whole hour!"

From a back room, the owner's voice quickly came to Maneta's rescue before she and the attendant went into their usual exchange, but not without Maneta throwing the usual reminder that if she had enough money, she had the nerve to stay on the computer for up to five hours. She also noted that one day she would have her own laptop and pay for her own internet service which she would enjoy from the comfort of her home without the misfortune to bump into good-for-nothing people like the attendant.

At home in her bed, Maneta found time to think over her cyber encounter with her new Facebook friend. The most outstanding aspect of her memory of him was his unfinished sentence before the computer logged her out and turned blank blue.

What was he trying to say before the screen froze? Was it for her to hear what he had to say about her pictures on her wall? Maneta always wanted to know what her male friends thought of her many pictures on her Facebook wall. In fact, she had just uploaded a few photos before she saw the red prompter alerting her to a new request for friendship. She had quickly clicked on it, and up came the friend, but with no photo on his profile. She was always displeased to have to see a blank wall when men requested friendships with her online.

Her first question to him, after accepting his friendship, was where he lived apart from the virtual world. It was in the country of her dreams! *America!* She felt pleased to confirm it in the name she preferred: *the USA?*

"Yes, in the USA," her new friend typed.

"What state?" she asked.

"New York."

"Wow! I love New York."

"Have you been to New York before?"

"No, I have never been out of my country!" She quickly typed a
if to erase some mistake she might have made to her new friend
Then she added, "What nationality are you?"

"I am a Virtualite!"

"You are funny," Maneta responded. "What nationality i
Virtualite?"

"I come from the back waters of the UN Building in Manhattan."

"*Mmmm*, that's fine for you," Maneta wrote, smiling. "Tha
should make you an American."

That was the conversation that had taken place between them ir
the five minutes they had become friends on Facebook. But she
did not readily show any eagerness for the new friendship. Like
she had done for the many others with whom she was eithe:
currently chatting or had chatted with before she *unfriended* them
for wasting her time and the little credit she struggled to raise tc
pay to access the Internet. Men are all the same, she maintained
They always want to discuss the sexuality of women. All of the
friends she had made, both the ones she initiated and the one:
who came after her, had insisted on her taking photos of hei
nudity, and posting them to their personal email addresses. These
men came from all over the world: black men, white men, browr
men, and even men without any proper racial colors.

She hadn't realized how deeply buried she was in thought abou:
her newfound cyber friend until her door was rudely kicked anc
was startled. A lady, in the worst of moods entered and stooc
firmly on her legs with arms on her hips as she hissed.

"I am not leaving without my money!" she barked.

"*Umu!* You don't have to do this. I will pay you as soon as I have
the money," Maneta pleaded.

"Every day you will pay me...you will pay me. *Me?* I cannot accep:
that today *oh*! I too have my own problems. It is three weeks now.
Each tme I ask, you lie to me that someone is sending you money
from abroad. *Today,* I need my money. You have money to go and

pay Bampia to enter his Internet, but you don't have money to pay me."

"What's your own in my internet business?

"I need my money *oh*, or I will not leave this place today."

"I don't have money today *oh*; you have to wait until I go to town tomorrow and come back."

"Maneta, I cannot wait another minute."

"But I don't have it now."

"You'd have to give me my money."

Umu dashed for the only valuable shoes that Maneta had and was making her way out when Maneta reached for the door and shut it before her. They struggled for some time until they ripped one of the shoes apart. Maneta, frustrated, fell on the floor and cried like a baby. Satisfied that she had made a point about how desperate she was for her money, Umu dropped one of the pair, and dashed out of the door with the other, swearing that Maneta would not have the other shoe until every penny of the debt was paid off.

Maneta lived with her daughter in a backyard room. The compound was crowded with tenants, including Umu. At least ten one-room apartments were littered all over the unkempt compound. The atmosphere was a stench from the outside toilet. Whenever there was mass cooking, the atmosphere became extremely suffocating by the mixed aroma from the single shared kitchen. Maneta's five-year old daughter only came into her room to sleep at night. She roamed the compound all day in the company of other kids. Luckily for them in the compound, all mothers were one mother, and one mother was all mothers.

Maneta did not cry because of the shoe that Umu ripped, but because on that day she had no penny to her name. She was hungry, her daughter was hungry, and she had spent the last penny she had to access the Internet. An Indonesian Facebook friend had faithfully promised her that because she had sent him the image he wanted to see of her, she was now entitled to his generosity. When she logged in the next time, she would receive a message with a code and directions on how to collect a fifty dollar note from an exchange bureau in town. The message never showed up nor was the Indonesian friend signed in. The only consolation she had, if it was ever a consolation, was meeting with the new friend who said he was a Virtualite.

She heard a knock on the door. A male voice introduced himself, but she did not show any excitement. She however invited him in. Abibu entered her room. Abibu had been a long time relationship that though he loved Maneta, but because he had not been able to provide enough for her, their relationship was strained. He stood for a while before helping himself to a corner of the bed. For a moment he was silent, and Maneta did not demonstrate any interest in having a conversation. Abibu heard Maneta's daughter crying outside. He quickly dashed out and returned with the child. It was then Maneta raised her head to make conversation as if she had only noticed him then. Abibu took a piece of bread from his handbag and gave it to the child, who, in accepting it, also accepted his pacification to stop crying. He took the child and put her on his lap. Between sobs and hiccups, the child began to chew the bread. After a while, Abibu allowed the child to come down from his lap. Maneta gave her some water to drink and allowed her to dash out in high spirits, to play with the other children outside. Maneta shut the door after her and returned to the bed.

"What do you want with us?" she asked.

"Why are you asking that? You know I was away visiting the village and I just returned to hear you and Umu fighting over nothing."

"I didn't think you cared. If you cared, you would want to know that I had nothing to eat at home before you went AWOL."

Abibu chuckled before he next spoke. "But you know that my wife…"

"*Ah! Ah!* I don't want to hear anything about your wife, please!"

Abibu shut up.

After a brief while, he dipped his hands into his pockets and retrieved a wad of notes. "This is for you."

Maneta sluggishly accepted the money. Her eyes widened in surprise, because it was such an impressive bundle.

"Hay, na watin dem dae kill tiday?" And she sat upright beaming with a smile as she examined the wad.

Abibu leaned back on the bed as he stared at the ceiling. Maneta embraced him.

"I have repaid Umu the money you owed her; and here is your shoe that she took from you."

"Na wae you get plenty for waste na dat make!" Maneta sucked on her teeth at length, detaching herself from Abibu in mock anger.

"She asks me for money, and I don't treat her like that. Why should she treat me like I am an un-paying debtor?"

"Okay, forget about it now."

Abibu edged himself properly on the bed to be at par with Maneta who still rested her head on the upper pillow. The two of them smiled at each other before Abibu slid under the sheets to join her.

Maneta paid for thirty minutes and was given a computer shortly after another client had vacated it. She signed her temporary entry code and opened her Facebook page. The internet was slow, but she was ready to wait forever. After a while, she was finally on Facebook. None of the messages was from her new friend. She decided to open the messages she had received. Suddenly, the icon for her new friend's message box popped up. Excitedly, she clicked on it.

"You slept with someone yesterday," the message read. "With a dark man," it added.

Maneta giggled, her face contorting. She quickly turned and looked around to see if anyone was reading her screen or reading her mind.

"What does this mean?" she typed.

"I mean you had sex with a man yesterday at your place."

"Are you joking or what?" she typed again.

"*Ahaahahaha!* I got you!"

"Why would you even think about that?" Maneta questioned.

"Because I know when people I care about cheat on me."

"You are funny. You and I don't even know each other yet."

"I know you now, even though you are not using the same computer in which we met."

"Oh, *please.* How could you know that?"

"I just know."

"Oh, I know, you are one of those I.T. geeks whose lives are all computers, right?"

"That's our life in Virtual Land."

"*Virtual Land* indeed," she typed, instinctively rolling her eyes.

Now comfortable with the conversation, she convinced herself that her new friend had to be the funny kind of guy. She even poked a joke at him that she knew he was sitting in his cozy room with an American girl. The new friend didn't respond to her on that. Instead when his message came again, it was to enquire as to why she had so many photos on Facebook.

"Oh, oh, someone is getting jealous!" Maneta replied.

The chatting continued the funny thread it started. Maneta was engrossed and kept smiling, at times even laughing aloud, drawing other clients' attention to herself. Each moment, Maneta, becoming more comfortable, chatted about everything she ever imagined America to be. She wanted to know about the kind of grass that grew there and the type of earth that made up the ground; she wanted to know about African Americans. She wanted to know what he had for breakfast, and what he was going to have for dinner; she wanted to know whether he had a big car, the likes that she always saw driven by 'big men', around Freetown. Finally, she told him she was eager to know what he looked like.

"Don't you know what I look like after all this while?" her friend questioned.

"How can I know when your picture is not on your page?"

"Are you sure it is not there? Go to my profile."

Maneta clicked to access his profile. At once there was the faint image of an innocent face, the most attractive face of any man she had ever seen. His eyes glowed with what appeared to be a golden dust of stars. They looked romantic, but at the same time intimidating. She felt as though his eyes transmitted an electrifying shock into her, creating an intense feeling of fatigue all over her body. Maneta intermittently had to avoid his eyes. It was as if they were drying up the wetness in her eyes. She convinced herself that her new friend could only be described as *a beautiful man*.

Just then, the computer screen blinked, and returned with the blue sky, and with the now irritating command for her to sign in anew. She hit the desk with her fist. And just as she was about to leave the seat, the computer hissed. She heard it but she did not pay any attention to it; all she was trying to avoid was the attendant's badmouthing. However, as she rose, the hissing sounded a little louder. She saw the screen playing between colors, and then, her Facebook page reappeared.

Her friend's message came through. Hesitantly, she stared closely at the screen as if she were only seeing it for the first time. Then, peering about her, she slowly returned to her seat.

Her friend had to be a computer wizard indeed! She had heard about those I.T. experts who could hack through any hidden passwords, access any computer and destroy them with viruses. This was going to be a good game on that good-for-nothing attendant who would not leave her in peace.

"Don't ask me how I did it, just go on and chat with me."

"I am not going to ask you any question on this one. That should be a good one, Mr. I.T. Wizard."

"I'm glad you know my name. I am the Wizard of Oz."

"Is that your nickname?"

"No, it is my real name."

"Ok, Mr. Hardy let's play the game."

"Oh yeah, let's play."

From the corner of her eyes, Maneta saw the attendant passing by her desk. She tried to ignore him while wondering whether he might have realized what had happened to the computer she was using, but the attendant only slowly walked by and instead went to trouble a nearby client. Why hadn't he bothered her that her thirty minutes were over—to think that he was not even countenancing her? What was pushing him away from her? Usually, if she had managed to buy credit for an hour, he would taunt her after the first thirty minutes, exactly when it was running past it. And here she was, two hours later, and still the attendant, going past her several times did not even, as much as tap her shoulder.

"You are lucky I have taken the attendant off your back."

"Wait a minute, how come you know everything happening around me? I hope you are not in one of the operating offices spying on me?"

"I told you I am the Wizard of Oz."

"You are right," Maneta responded.

"Now baby, tell me, how does one go to your place?"

"Don't you know, Mr. Wizard? So, after all, there are many things you don't know."

They chatted for another hour, mostly bordering on the romantic. Wiz displayed many more pictures of himself. Each photo mesmerized Maneta more than the previous ones. How lucky she was, she thought, that she should not only have met a friend residing in the country of her dreams, but a man who more than fitted her desire. Luckier was she even more that she had met a friend who was eager to chat with her anytime; a friend who was not interested in asking for photos of her nudity. After about three hours on the Internet, she signed off. Instantly, the attendant dashed to Maneta's desk and mocked her about the expiration of her thirty minutes.

Thirty minutes? Was this attendant stupid, or was he away all this while?

She was shocked when the attendant even commended her for using the computer for exactly thirty minutes. In shock, but also lost in her memory of the company she had kept with Wiz, she advised herself to merely ignore the buffoonery and hasten out of the café.

At the exit of the café, she caught sight of a lady jumping around in an excited mood. She remembered her as a fellow patron at the café, although they had never made an acquaintance. Smiling to herself, Maneta soon realized that the lady must have just gotten some good news. As she exited the door, she felt warm hands tapping her shoulder. She turned and held the beaming face of the cheerful lady.

"I have got it, the ticket and the visa! I am going to America!" the lady screamed.

By this time, three other ladies had joined her jubilation. Although Maneta was openly happy for her, she was baffled as to why the lady had brought her into the matter.

"Party time at the beach, and you are invited! We are off to the beach. Food and drinks are on me. My boyfriend has done it for me, and so I have to celebrate tonight."

Maneta was just about to thank her for the invitation, and to assure her that even though she would not be making it, she was truly happy for her, when the lady shoved her ticket and her passport into her hands.

"Take a look! There you will find the green design of the American visa!"

Maneta looked at it keenly. Was Wiz going to bring such happiness to her face? The jubilant lady held Maneta by the hand and pulled her into the taxi she'd just summoned. The taxi took off at high speed leaving a cloud of dust behind it.

The nightclub was already crowded by the time Maneta and the other ladies arrived. A stench of cigarette smoke was in the air and music was at high volume. The dance floor sweated with the perspiration of the dancers. There were jubilations and congratulations followed by several snapshots. One girl walked up to Maneta, and without the formalities of a new acquaintance brought out a picture from her handbag and showed it to her.

"Do you think this is a nice picture to send to my boyfriend?" the girl enquired.

Maneta looked at it closely as if she were scrutinizing it for faults. "But you wouldn't send this picture with someone to give to your boyfriend. It will quickly pass around from one hand to another, and people will see all of that body of yours."

"No, I'm not giving it to anyone. I'm in-boxing it to my boyfriend's Facebook message—for his eyes only. Nannette sent many of these to her guy before the ticket came running for her to go to the USA." The girl said, returning the picture to her bag. "If they don't see, they don't buy. People here don't know good things. He is a white guy. His dad worked here many years ago as a Peace Corp. He said he would be glad to take a wife from here." She took out the picture of the white man. "Lookie! Lookie! We became Facebook friends some three months ago, and already he is paying my rents. He lives in Manhattan, New York."

Manhattan! Maneta's heart missed a beat. She quickly looked at the white man's picture again before she concluded that it was not her Wiz. Should she really send this kind of picture to Wiz Hardy. She had done it before, but it did not yield her any dividend; in fact, the Indonesian fellow did not even get back to her. Then she suddenly remembered that Wiz had commented, rather disdainfully, about her having too many pictures on Facebook. But before she became deeply lost in thought, the jubilant lady pulled her by the hand unto the dance floor.

It was past midnight when Maneta arrived home. Her apartment's compound was quiet and dark when she stepped into it. She stole her way through the rugged surface. Her daughter should be fast asleep at her neighbor's. She decided that she should let her alone and pick her up in the morning. Her neighbor wouldn't mind. She was sure of that. She therefore went directly to her door, but just as she was turning her key, her neighbor's door flew open.

"Maneta, I did not want this to wait until tomorrow," the neighbor said.

Maneta stopped fidgeting with her key. "I didn't want to wake you up only to collect my baby. I thought it was best to wait till morning. Hope she didn't cause you much trouble?"

The neighbor moved closer since it was dark and the two couldn't make out each other from the distance. Maneta noticed that she carried something in her hands.

"Is she still asleep?"

"This is not your baby. I received this package on your behalf this evening," her neighbor said.

"A package! From where?"

"How do I know? I wish I could read like you. The world's most handsome man brought it for you."

"Did he say his name?"

"He didn't say a word. He gave me a pen to sign, and when I told him I couldn't read and write, he produced a soft pad and I dipped my thumb and pressed it on his book. He gave me the parcel and left—it was more like he disappeared. His eyes were something else. They left me cold and weak," she chuckled. "Don't allow me to bore you. You must be tired and would want to know what you have in that parcel. Don't worry about your daughter; you can pick her up in the morning. She is sound asleep."

All tiredness had gone from Maneta. Her eyes were now excited to discover what was in the parcel. When she entered her apartment, she reached for the hurricane lamp and lit it. She returned to her parcel. It had come from the USA! And indeed, her eyes were beholding the name of Wiz Hardy. She quickly tore open the parcel, and there surfaced a beautiful Dell laptop. Her heart missed a beat, another beat, and another beat. Her breath paused. She fell back on her chair. It was then that an exuberant excitement overwhelmed her, and she burst out with happiness She returned to the parcel and discovered that other equipment was enclosed. There was a mobile modem to access the Internet. There was a spare battery for the laptop. A short note was tacked to the cover of the laptop. *This is to make your dream come true. That obnoxious Internet café attendant will never see you again. Enjoy your toy.* Signed, Wiz-Hard!

After fidgeting with the parcel for a while, Maneta dashed to her room. While in her room, she was sure that she heard the rustling of the packet that was wrapped around the laptop. She carefully picked her steps to the door. She peeped. There on the floor, playing with the torn packet was her daughter. How could her neighbor just drop her daughter off after she had promised to keep her until daybreak? What was the meaning of this? The baby looked at her and laughed. Maneta picked her up and kissed her, and told her not to mind aunty. She was probably dashing off to attend to a matter that couldn't just wait. She reached for the front door, but discovered to her utter surprise, that the door remained as neatly closed with the key as she had locked it on entering.

She fainted!

A blue glow appeared in the center of the laptop and after a while it began to increase in size. Maneta's daughter, who had sat crying after her mother had fainted, became attracted to the glow. She slowly moved toward the laptop. Meanwhile the glow kept increasing in size and its brightness took over the room. By the time Maneta's daughter reached the laptop, the glow had brightened to the point of spreading rays through the eaves of the door to the darkness outside.

In a while, a soft jingle began to play; the screen began changing into many other colors, ebbing and flowing like a sea. Three big bubbles appeared on the screen, rolling about. Maneta's daughter put out her left hand, attempting to capture one of the bubbles. She enjoyed the trying to catch the bubbles, giggling as they kept eluding her fingers. She then thrust both hands at the screen. In that instant, the bubbles disappeared. The jingle stopped. The glow receded. Maneta's daughter's hands remained glued to the screen. She cried, unable to detach her hands. Then her hand sank into the screen, then her head, and eventually her entire body.

In that instant, Maneta gained consciousness, just as the laptop shut itself and the glow disappeared, leaving a dark screen. Though she felt an excruciating migraine, she managed to stagger on her legs, screaming as she dashed for the door. However, before she could reach the door, the glow appeared in its full force, and divided into two ropes of flames, wrapping around Maneta's sides. She had succeeded in opening the door and fought hard to free herself from the grips of the flaming ropes. The flames of ropes began trembling like leaves in the wind. Then multiple colors changed, at first in gradual glow and then screwing into different colors in rapid succession. The ropes themselves began to throw her from one side of the room to the other until she too was eventually swallowed into the laptop's screen.

Maneta felt her body floating in dark air. She felt the chilly sensation of being suspended. Then she experienced being lowered gradually until her feet touched the ground. The atmosphere was rather foggy just as her mind was.

As soon as her feet touched the ground, a door appeared before her. She walked through it without knowing where she was going. Bright lights appeared that took away the fog from her eyes. She kept running into doors as though someone was after her. Once, twice, three doors ahead of her, each leading to nowhere. Then suddenly, the ground gave way from under her and she fell through a wide abyss into a dark room. She remained still in the dark. Before long a blue glow appeared in the center of the room and began to increase in size.

The room became fully bright and Maneta was able to decipher the image of a hanging human being. She soon realized that it was her daughter. Mechanically, she screamed and dashed for her, but each time she forced her way towards her daughter, the glowing light would pull Maneta back. However, she kept assuring her daughter that she was going to be okay.

"We do not want your child, and we do not intend to hurt her, if only you can stop screaming and listen to what I have to communicate to you," a voice said to her.

She could not place any face to it. "Whoever you are, why are you doing this to me and my daughter? Let her go, let her go please. Don't hurt her."

"Very well, Maneta," The figure behind the voice appeared before her.

"Wiz Hardy!"

"*Ah, ah*, Wizard, not Wiz Hardy. Did you have a good trip to my USA? Follow me, Maneta."

Wiz automatically turned around and began walking through a door. As he moved, Maneta's hanging daughter began to follow him in the air. It was then that Maneta got up and followed them. She increased her speed and tried to grab her daughter from the air.

"I wouldn't do that. Your daughter is hanging on a slim invisible thread—the thread of her own life. If you as much as touch her the thread would cut and she would die."

They came to a big open place. A flat elevated alter was burning bright with candles on all four sides of it. Wiz turned to Maneta and invited her to sit with him at table. He informed her that she was in Virtual Land, a land that had been invaded by people of her kind. And since her kind was now more connected with each other on Virtual Land, war had to be declared over mankind.

"But Wiz, you are yourself human—you look like me and I look like you. Look how real you are. Why can't we all just live as one?" Maneta tried to reason.

"That's the problem with you humankinds. You think that anyone wearing this frame is a human. This is exactly why you humans are limited in everything: in wisdom, in capacity and in lifespan. Your frame is a prison. I am in this frame only because I am here to engage you. Remember when I had to show you a photograph of myself on Facebook? It was to help you control your thoughts of what I might look like, but I do not necessarily look like the fellow you are seeing right now."

"What do you mean by that? Is this not you that I am seeing right now?" Maneta asked.

"That's as much as you can see of me for as long as you remain to be only a human being. But there are many sides of me, and that's the wonderful thing about being a Virtualite. In addition to what we are and unlike you human beings, we do not die."

"Why then are you threatened by us human beings? You can live forever. You are vampires."

"We are not vampires—even they are limited just like you are," Wiz said.

"In that case, every living organism has to have a limitation. You Virtualites have to have your own limitations."

At this point a protean anger boiled inside of Wiz. Maneta's reasoning hurt him so badly that he had to yell a big and long '*No!*' at her. He reasoned with her that only living beings that do not have the potential to be divisible could speak of limitations.

"You don't get it. We live forever!" Wiz was raging.

"And you don't live on pepper and salt, is it?" Maneta showed her doubts.

"We are going to rule your world and that's the truth!" Wiz shouted.

He was still speaking angrily when he told her that he was going to demonstrate the Virtualite's power of being divisible, even as a single entity. Immediately, a gushing wind, coming from nowhere, began to spin around them at a high speed.

After the strange wind had spiraled around Wiz for a few minutes, his human form began to detach from his main frame: the head detached from the neck and hung itself just above the main frame. It was still communicating with Maneta. Then the hands detached and hung in the air considerably away from the body. The legs swept themselves from under and joined the hands. The torso began rotating in the whirlwind. While this was going on, Wiz assured Maneta that because he did not originally exist as a human body, all she was seeing at that moment was for her to understand what he meant by virtual divisibility. He then went ahead and changed each of the human forms into something else. Among the changes there appeared a big rock, a sea fish and a tree. Still engaging Maneta, he asked her to think of any object that she wanted him to change into. Maneta was unwilling at first, but after being urged, named as many as ten objects into which Wiz changed before he returned to his human form. The wind died down immediately after that.

At that same instant, Maneta's daughter slowly descended to the ground. Maneta grabbed her and began to run away. She ran back through the doors that she had entered. But wherever she ran, Wiz appeared in front of her. She began pleading with him not to harm them. She saw an opening on her right, and as Wiz surged forward to seize her, she escaped into the opening. It was a rather long opening. She and her daughter rolled on a long ride in which, like a ball, the ride took them from one inlet and outlet, each time throwing them before being deposited on a heap of rubbish. Grabbing her daughter, she quickly took to her heels. Although she didn't know where she was running, she kept running very fast, as long as she got away from Wiz.

But soon a familiar voice began to call her name. She decided to risk stopping to enquire who it was. To her amazement, it was Abibu. *How could he have got here?* She wondered whether to trust him or not and decided that in her current situation no one was to be trusted. She reached for a fat log nearby and took a confrontational posture as Abibu approached her.

"Abibu, stop there! Why are you here?"

But Abibu kept advancing.

"I need you to stop right there." She held firmly to her daughter.

Abibu stood still. "What is going on here, Maneta? How come I'm here in this place? I was in your room a few minutes ago, how come you and I are here?"

Maneta realized that Abibu was as confused as she was. She lowered the log and Abibu came up to her and held her in his arms. Maneta began to sob.

"Something is happening to us. I don't know what."

"This has to be some evil force. Don't worry, we are going to try to get out of here," Abibu assured her. "What is that thing in your room with the bright light that blinded me? After calling your phone and not receiving a response, I visited your place. The door was shut. It took a hammer to open it. Some force pulled me in and then there was this bluish bright light that blinded me, and I became unconscious. When I gained consciousness, I found myself here," Abibu reported.

Maneta spared herself explaining the entire story of the laptop. "That's the same mysterious happening that landed me and my daughter here."

In that instant, a loud sound came from behind them. They heard horse hooves approaching. Abibu grabbed Maneta's daughter as they all ran into hiding. The noise grew louder and louder. From their hiding place, they were able to see the procession of Virtualites passing by. They all had on heavy armored dresses and straight faces as they marched along.

"That's the population in the entire Virtual Land," a voice came from behind them.

Maneta and Abibu swiftly turned around and grabbed whatever they found and began to hit the man behind them. All the time he kept pleading that he was not one of them; he was a human being. They stopped beating him.

"Momodu, the name's Momodu Cole. They have kept me here for two years now. I am of no use to them, that's why they don't go after me."

Maneta narrated her encounter with Wiz and all that he had told her about himself. She also told them how he changed into the many objects that came to her head.

"He lied to you when he told you that Virtualites don't have a limitation," Momodu said.

"Yeah, he told me that they were unlimited in everything," Maneta remembered.

"I don't know where Virtualites come from, but the entire population is not more than ten thousand in number. Yes, they don't die, that's true, but something else is bothering them. They are never able to be you…I mean they have tried to impersonate us, but they cannot. They will always be ten thousand in number, no more, no less, because they do not reproduce their kind."

"Why is that a problem? I don't care to live forever and don't have to reproduce my kind," Abibu said.

"That's true only if we, humans did not exist," said Momodu.

"How's that?" Maneta asked.

"Well, for one thing we have invaded their space. All the millions of viewers on Facebook, twitter, Tagged, Bing and all those chat sites have made life miserable for the Virtualites."

Momodu stood up. "Follow me," he said.

The three of them walked out of their hiding place. Abibu took Maneta's daughter by the hand.

Casting his eyes about, Momodu said, "Look at this place, see how miserable the atmosphere is. When I was swallowed last year, this place had life. Virtualites could be seen all over the place socializing. But look at it now," he paused. "Their lives are now haunted by six billion earth people.

He paused for a while and continued, "That explains why any earth woman could be brought here. They want to experiment with infusing their genes into the human system to see if that could bring about a new species with seventy percent virtual genes and thirty percent human genes. They reckon that when this new person is sent back to earth, and mates, a Virtualite child will be born."

Maneta and the others saw an object falling from the sky. As it descended on them, it changed midair into a human form. There stood Wiz before them clapping his hands.

"Momodu, you have done well. What a good lesson on the limitation of Virtualites. You got it right; we Virtualites are the creation of the internet age. Yes, we do not reproduce. But when you say we will always remain ten thousand in number, there you have told the biggest untruth," he paced around them in a circlular motion. "You see, the very things that create problems for you are the things you can use to solve the problems."

"But no one has created any problems for you and your kind," Maneta shouted.

Wiz ignored her. "Human beings believe that they are the center of creation. But the truth is that while you may be the center of your own universe, you fail to understand that there are thousands of other universes where you do not matter. Millions of you have taken the pleasure of washing your dirty linens on cyber space, where we Virtualites are in the center of creation. Our lives have become miscrable because of your Facebook, Handbooks, Footbooks and all those other chat rooms you have created."

"But you are only ten thousand in number and you cannot fight us who are six billion and counting...don't you get that?" Maneta shouted again.

"Oh yeah," Wiz immediately took offense. "Don't I get it? What don't I get? I have tried to impress it on your mind that Virtualites are superior to you mortals. What don't I get? That you and your kind are a suffering miserable lot who have to eat every day to survive? Who are just limited in those frames of yours?"

"We are reasonable beings. Where we come from, we strive to live in peace with each other," Abibu jumped in. "If you have issues with us your authorities can simply contact our earth authorities, and everything can be worked out for everyone's good."

"Virtualites do not have singular authorities over us. We all think like leaders, and so whatever I do here is the same any other Virtualite would do. You people need authorities because you are primitive and uncivilized. Speaking of which, I have a surprise for you." The Wiz turned away from them and spoke in a foreign dialect, and then in English, "Earthman, come forward."

A man covered in armor from head to toe, walked from behind a wall and marched directly to Wiz. Wiz examined him for a while before passing a next command in the strange dialect. Instantly the armor began opening from the feet all the way up to expose a human being.

"What?! What is the meaning of this?" Maneta shouted. "What have you done to him?"

"You are not mistaken, Maneta. You are certainly seeing a superior version of the attendant at the café you used to visit to access the Internet," Wiz beamed with joy. "You can refer to him as Earthman. He is half Virtual, half Earth. He has a mission. He is our first experiment of future Earthmen who would help Virtualites reproduce. Earthman has been programmed to mate with you Maneta, and to reproduce the completely new Virtualites!"

"You are mad!" Maneta shouted.

Earthman, formerly known to Maneta as the café attendant, continued to stand still as stone.

"No, madness is for human beings," Wiz responded. "Sorry, Earth People, this conversation is over. Earthman, you have the power, Maneta Bongay is your mate. Go after her and make us Virtual babies!" He uttered a broad echoing laugh as he took off into the air, changing into many objects before disappearing in the distance.

Earthman took two steps forward and demanded the hand of Maneta by stretching out his own hand. Momodu, who had been quiet for most of the exchange, stepped forward to bar the way. They eyed each other with hostility for a while before Earthman elbowed him. Momodu was flung into the air before he crashed in the nearby dump. Earthman continued to advance on Maneta, who by now was cupping her daughter to her chest. Abibu uttered something unintelligible and confronted Earthman, lending his whole weight against him. Earthman staggered three steps backward, before hitting Abibu and sending him sprawling on the ground. Abibu and Momodu held tight fists as they both rushed at Earthman. Earthman reeled back from the blows and fell over in a heap. He quickly recovered and advanced on both men. He gave a solid kick to Abibu, again sending him rolling on his back. When Momodu took a stick and attempted to hit Earthman, he pulled an object from his right side and sprayed fire at him. Momodu cried aloud as he went crashing down and burning to death.

By now Maneta had grabbed her daughter and ran down a runway. Earthman followed her. Abibu also followed behind them. The chase took them from one alleyway to another. Earthman sprayed fire at every structure and blowed up anything in his way. Abibu threw objects at Earthman to distract him from Maneta and her daughter. When Abibu persisted with his actions, this angered Earthman, who then turned his attention to Abibu. This gave Maneta and her daughter an opportunity to hide away. Abibu had also hidden himself.

Earthman turned around looking for him and slowed down at the end of one alleyway. Abibu who held a big net in his hand aimed for Earthman's head and dropped it on him. The net covered him all the way down to his feet. While he fought to remove it, Abibu shoved him and he tumbled over and rolled down the alleyway. Abibu then ran down to the other end to where Maneta had gone to hide. They quickly embraced. By the time they released each other, Maneta's daughter had disappeared. They broke off searching for her but none of the immediate locations yielded anything of her. Maneta began sobbing.

They separated to search for her. Abibu stopped and looked again before he shouted for Maneta to come over to him. Maneta rushed over to where he was standing. Abibu pointed and Maneta followed the direction with her eyes. Below where they stood and in the middle of fire-gutted structures sat Earthman with Maneta's daughter cupped in his hands. Maneta ran down the hill, pulling her hair and hurling threats of what she would do to Earthman if he did anything to her baby. Her threatening voice degenerated to crying. Abibu ran closely behind. When they reached Earthman, they stopped.

Maneta negotiated, "Please, please don't hurt my baby…she is only just a baby."

Earthman's head was bowed and the little girl played and laughed.

"Baby, you are going to be alright…just you hold on,.Mama is going to get you from him," Maneta comforted her daughter.

"I don't think he means any harm to the baby, look, he is just giving her a gentle stroking."

"How can you say so, this thing just brought down this whole place and killed Momodu."

"I am not going to hurt your daughter, I am not."

"You see, I told you," Abibu took Maneta by the hand, pacifying her.

A few seconds passed before Earthman raised his head to look at Maneta and Abibu. Maneta did not remember ever beholding such a mangled and patched up figure. The only evidence that proved that she stood before the man she used to know as the attendant at the café she frequented was his face. Hesitantly, she moved closer and closer to him.

"Maneta, this is me, the guy who used to trouble you at the café. Look how miserable I am," he began to sob.

"It's going to be okay. Let's try to get out of here."

Maneta tried to help Earthman to his knees but the effort was futile. He asked Abibu to help, but the effort was still futile. Earthman continued to sob, seeking to know how much destruction he had caused under the spell of the Virtualites. Maneta wanted him to control his emotions so she told him how much power he used to destroy huge giant buildings and how he had killed an innocent poor man who had only come to her aid

"You must restrain yourself from killing your fellow human beings and instead try to get us from this wretched situation," Maneta reasoned with him.

"Go!" Earthman uttered.

"Go?" Maneta questioned.

"Yes, go. The Virtualites are out searching for me. They are on their way here."

Maneta grabbed her baby and together with Abibu hid behind a thick wall.

"Don't you people go too far. I promise to rescue you and send you back to Earth,

From where Maneta hid, she saw four Virtualites approach Earthman. They spoke to him, examined him and took him off in a stretcher. He had been badly wounded. Maneta and Abibu watched until the stretcher was out of sight. They sat on the floor, realizing for the first time, since the beginning of their ordeal, that they had not had any food or drink of any kind. Five minutes later they were sprawled on the floor, fast asleep.

Maneta felt a cold touch on her arm. Startled from her sleep, she opened her mouth to scream. Earthman immediately covered her mouth to stop her from screaming. He told them to follow him at once. Hesitantly they stole into the dark behind Earthman. Walking into endless darkness, Maneta and Abibu took turns at carrying the baby on their shoulders. When they came to a particular spot, Earthman shouted for them to stop a little away from him.

"I have been given more Virtualite genes in my system and unless we can send you off quickly, I will turn against you and seek to destroy you. Do not waste any more time. Do as I tell you and you will be gone from this place. If I can escape from here, I shall be coming to Earth soon—after all I am Earthman."

That little bit was meant as a joke to ease the tension, but there were no nerves left for fun in Maneta and Abibu. Earthman knelt and opened a vault. It was an empty vault with only a bright bluish light.

"Now all of you get in here," Earthman ordered.

Maneta and Abibu hesitated.

"Trust me on this one—but that trust may not be for too long before I change to my Virtualite self."

First to go was Abibu, before Maneta, thanking Earthman, stepped into the vault with her daughter strapped to her back. Earthman looked at them and wished them good luck. But just as he was shutting the vault, he felt a spasm. He yelled into the thick black night as he broke off the lid, and stretched his hand to grab Maneta by the hair. He roared and roared and called on other Virtualites to stop the escape of Maneta and her daughter. Maneta and Abibu struggled to close the vault with the broken lid. They could hear more voices approaching. It was getting too late for them before the lid finally fitted and swallowed the night and took off into the air.

Maneta, her daughter and Abibu materialized in her room, flying through space and time. Dumbfounded, they searched around in disbelief. Everything in her room was as she recalled leaving it. The laptop still sat on the table, harmless and cold. Except for the door that had been broken in. How was she to tell this story? Who was going to believe anyway? Meanwhile her daughter cried for food.

"I think I should go out and look for something to eat," Abibu offered.

"No, don't go, I should. Let me find out what people are saying," Maneta said.

She stepped out of the door. There were the usual noises of housemates cooking and doing other chores. At first nobody seemed to take any notice of her. She felt her body, touching herself over as if to to confirm she was visible. She proceeded to a housemate whom she requested from and received a bowl of newly cooked rice. She quickly walked back to her room. Was it that nobody knew what she had gone through? She returned to the room only to meet Abibu staring at the laptop. He was so engrossed in it that he didn't hear her inviting him to have some food.

"You might want to take a look at this," Abibu said.

"That computer again! I need to get rid of it."

"Not so fast. Come and take a look at this," Abibu insisted.

"This is who you know as Earthman. I sent you this message before I let you into the vault. Please keep your laptop with you, I shall communicate with you anything I want you to know. But for now, please alert the authorities that the Virtualites are about to bring doom to earth."

That night while Abibu was sound asleep, Maneta took the laptop and dumped it in the toilet outside. Her life and that of her daughter couldn't be brought into this madness. She returned to sleep. Several days passed before she decided that her life and that of her child had returned to normal. She had no intention of going near any café just yet. That no one seemed to know anything about her ordeal made her believe that she, her daughter and Abibu would have been bewitched if it were not for the intervention of God. Church became her foremost preoccupation. The devil had to be cast out by all means.

After confessing in church that her previous life of greed and love of money had made her a target of the devil, she agreed with the congregation that only praying ceaselessly could bring back her stolen soul to the Lord. At night, lighted candles were her armor to keep the devil away. The Bible always neatly laid under her

pillow.   Only once did she remove it temporarily when it wa
obvious that she was going to make love to Abibu.   Not tha
Abibu believed that he and Maneta had been bewitched, but h
reasoned that it was best to follow in Maneta's line of thinking as
way of providing succor to her.

One night when it was not possible for Abibu to sleep over at he
place because his wife needed extra help, Maneta sang all the joyfu
songs of redemption that she had learned, backing them with
copious verses from the Bible. She went to sleep with the Bibl
under her head and three candles glowing in the center of th
room. The laptop appeared before her and she went into a barrage
of prayers to cast the devil off.

Earthman's message and the laptop stayed in the room: *unles
Maneta reported the matter to the political and military authorities, earth wa
doomed.* That night Maneta took her daughter, boarded a taxi anc
went to the church building where the pastor gave her a place tc
spend the night. However, the night refused to pass uneventfully
because Earthman wanted her to hear him out. She sought solace
in the toilet, the laptop went with her, in the garage, the laptop
went after her; finally in the vestry, the laptop went after her
Earthman reasoned out with her that if he were of the devil i
would all have stopped. Maneta finally gave up. At dawn, she
returned to her room where the computer was waiting for her, bu
this time it did not bother her.   Following a lengthy cybe
exchange, she agreed to approach the authorities? But which
authorities? Certainly not her church authorities. She knew now
that this was not a church matter.

However, after the police and the military had turned her down
and after the media and the civil society organizations had turned
her down, she returned to the church. The pastor agreed to
spearhead her 'final days' campaign. She tried to tell the pastor that
this was not a 'final days' campaign but a modern reality. The
pastor gathered the congregation and they threw their weight
behind her.

Before long, buildings were being blown up in central Freetown. The church became afraid of Maneta. Her pastor and his congregation quickly abandoned her, and in fact accused her of using the powers of Jezebel to cause mayhem. The media embraced her vehemently, articulating in detail anything she said that Earthman was telling her. Earthman wanted the Sierra Leone government to alert the American government to join forces in the fight against the Virtualites.

America and other countries ruled out any intervention into what they described as the country's civil war. The African Union and the Economic Community of West African States warned that they didn't have any more resources to help address a second war in Sierra Leone. Finally, Maneta had a message for America and all others who thought it was just a one country affair: *the Virtualites, numbered ten thousand immortals are now all over Africa and America.* Other African countries were reporting destructions with no enemies in sight. Every day the destruction was claiming the lives of citizens and property. No country could quell the destruction and the killing. Maneta became highly sought after: *What else was Earthman saying?*

The United States Government requested that since this war appeared to be a cyber space war, it would be helpful for Maneta to be where the technology to track down cyber communications was. Maneta and Earthman were suddenly the most important figures on Earth, as the world powers realized that with all their chemical and nuclear arsenals, they couldn't defeat the Virtualites.

While at NASA headquarters, Maneta picked up another signal from Earthman: *The whole world should agree to shut down every computer and laptop for forty-five minutes.* In that period, the Virtualites, who were only immortal while in Virtual Land, and could not survive on Earth for thirty minutes if they couldn't find powered-on computers to infiltrate, would disappear forever.

The American president needed to give his consent to turn off all computers in America—but a certain General was on record saying, "How can we allow a third-world sorcerer from Africa to instruct us on un-militaristic warfare? The whole of the civilized world is connected to the cyber world—Do Maneta and her Earthman know what that means?"

The world continued to look on as the death toll rose and the destructions continued. Then another American war general suggested that computers could be turned off regionally instead of all at once. The decision was accepted by war leaders, but no advice was sought from Maneta and Earthman.

All of Africa and Asia turned off their computers. Two hours later the destruction continued. All over where there were TV's, homes tuned and reluctantly, the leaders of America, Russia, China and other world powers met following pressure from their citizens to heed to Maneta's advice.

Virtualites, all computers, laptops and artificial energy were turned off from one end of the world to the other. The world waited…

The destruction sustained for thirty minutes before everywhere went silent.

The world waited for another hour and when there was no longer any destruction, it was declared that the military of every country should comb all areas as a last attempt to trap any remaining enemies. After three hours of that operation, all computers and energy operated machinery turned back on. The world had never suffered such human and material loss.

A PLACE TO DIE

What better place to draw one's last breath than in the house of God? Sengbe Pieh, ecclesiastical of thought, had settled. With such a resolve, as was always known of him, the only other matter to overcome was to conquer the seven-forest- -long journey, between the village square he had just arrived at and the missionary compound, the locals had reminded him was up the gradient hill.

The villagers' consternation, brought about by Sengbe Pieh's haggard and ghostly look, had made them resort to manifesting their disapproval and rejection of his presence in their midst until he felt the pangs of their disgust, and went on his way from them.

At the age of eighty something years, the inevitable footpath of seven forests was more of an ache in his mind than it was on his already pinching and bare soles when he resumed his journey. The bouts of agony posed the cruelest challenge to his desire to reach the missionary compound. Taking one peripheral step after another was even more grueling than the distance he had to cover.

As he began to walk away from the village, he realized with satisfaction that none of the locals knew who he really was. In the early months of his return from slavery in America, there was not a household in Sherbro and Mende lands that did not recognize him. He had grown tired of recalling those mundane moments, but only if his memory would help it. The sorrow of coming from the known hero to the unknown, even among his own people, from whom he was now fleeing, and seeking to find the church that had disowned him on his return to Africa, discomforted him like broken blades in his mouth.

In those early months of his return, just as everyone was clamouring to share the glory with him as the former Sherbro slave who had mutinied at sea, killed almost every one of his captors, went to America and legally as well as 'magically' gained his freedom from the white man, Sengbe Pieh had suddenly disappeared. He left to search for his wife and children, entrusting that information to no one.

When pain had buried for too long inside of one, particularly at a ripe old age, it would always be difficult not to smell conspiracy in every other full-blooded human being one crosses path with. For that matter, and the pains brought about by the absence of his family from Mende, Sengbe Pieh remained gloomy for the most part of his life on earth.

After he had first arrived at the village square, several forest of distance behind him, Sengbe Pieh had almost forgotten how much hunger had twisted his stomach when fatigue had forced him to slouch on the ground in the middle of the village square. Even before trying to know what creature he was, and where he was from, the villagers had informed him that there was nowhere to put him up, even for the night, neither was there any leftover food for him, and that the best there was for him to do was to pick up himself and leave before the uglier citizens of the village returned from hunting and missed him for a lingering haunt that must be quickly shot at for supper.

Haggard as he was, Sengbe Pieh had accepted that only the church could afford to look after his person until called to lie down with his ancestors. But what other option was there for a man, his age, and having drained all the blood of hope and energy from his bones, to find comfort at such an old age and a peaceful deathbed?

If he was doomed not to ever see his beloved family, his wife and three children again, then let him die in the comfort of the church. He was angry at first that he should opt to seek refuge in a church that had once betrayed him. Was it going to betray him again?

After a while, though, he had thought of the idea of seeking refuge in the church, an idea he had turned over in his mind, perhaps by the power of a miraculous spirit, he agreed with his own soul that only the church could bring about a dignified closure to his endless search for his family.

Sengbe Pieh was happy to realize that he eventually covered the seven-forest distance that led to the church. Already, the familiar tower with the cross of Jesus at its apex rose ahead of him. Even though he had not seen it for at least three decades, since he helped erect it upon his return from slavery, he still remembered the mystery behind the gold crest image of the cross and the twinkling silver star resting on its tip. That afternoon, when the young American missionary climbed up the ladder to affix the Silver Star on the tip of the cross, Sengbe Pieh thought he saw a lengthy ray of sunlight flashing across the Silver Star, and the missionary's hand trembled like a need.

As he approached the missionary compound, the feeling of that same holiness returned to him as he stood in front of the colossal gate. For a moment, he stood still and wondered whether he was clean enough to seek clemency in the house of God. Suddenly, he felt an intense sense of hesitation and backed away from the gate.

The only other time he had ever hesitated that much was in the schooner, the pirate ship that had stolen him from Komende. He remembered that after he and others had successfully unchained themselves at sea, and struggled with their between captors, a young Spanish lad, under the instruction of a drunken adult Spanish man, had taken a knife to stab Sengbe Pieh in his face. He had grabbed the boy by his throat and shoved him off. The boy was told to advance with a bigger knife thrown to him by the much older Spaniard. Sengbe Pieh had taken the boy down by his legs. Sengbe Pieh had kept the nail he had freed himself with over him. The boy could have been slightly older than his own son left in Africa. But with no sorrow, the boy had stabbed him. He had

groaned, and with all his might had dealt the boy a fatal blow. He
would never have killed the boy if it was not a matter of life and
death.

Brought back from his thoughts, a heavy shower dropped on
Sengbe Pieh, as if it was to further stop him from entering the
missionary compound. The noise of the rain was so deafening
that his loudest call and his hardest pounding on the door did not
bring anyone in response. He pounded again. Those who
eventually heard it did not come to his aid. Instead, they scared
him away from the door. A pack of dogs advanced at him so
voraciously that he took to his heels, seeking refuge in a nearby
hut, which also provided him shelter from the uncompromising
rain.

Pen, the young Black American Missionary in Komende, had
nearly finished having his supper when he thought he heard an
unusual noise. He stepped away from his dining table, still
chewing on a piece of mutton, holding an empty spoon in his
hand. He was only three weeks in Komende, and still regularly
startled by any noise he heard. He walked to the front door and
pressed his right ear to the door. Indeed, he could hear the sound
of banging on the gate outside.

It was dark outside and the wind was flailing. After a period of
initial shock, Pen suspected that most of the noises were those of
scavenging dogs barking, or some ritualistic pagan group
performing a ceremony somewhere far away. However, the
tormenting noise persisted and turned desperate.

The banging grew louder. And as been noted, in just three weeks
after his arrival in Africa, Pen was already used to rescuing helpless
locals from becoming fatal victims to some ritualistic lore. This
might very well be one of those cases, he thought. He opened the
door and was swallowed by the harsh arrows of a black rain.
Without picking up a torch, he ran to the watchman's shed,
shouting at the top of his voice to wake the man up from a dead

and deep sleep. The watchman was used to that kind of rude awakening from the young missionary ever since he was brought to the mission because it appeared that every day the gods wanted the villagers to offer sacrifices of animals or drum in their praises. He knew that any soul met at the gate was to be instantly rescued and dragged to the church of God. In an instant, he flung open the gate, and pulled the man who had been thumping on the gate into the compound. He guided the victim to the church and sat him in a pew.

Pen entered the church to be greeted by an old man.

"Who is our late night guest?" Pen questioned the watchman.

"I never knowed him, this man, and he nor look like anyone in the village. First time to see him meself, this man," the watchman said and began to excuse himself from Pen.

"Wait here, Joe," he told the watchman.

The watchman looked into Pen's face before retreating to a corner to wait.

"Old man, do you speak English?" Pen hesitantly advanced toward Sengbe Pieh. When Sengbe Pieh did not answer, Pen turned to the watchman and asked, "Did you talk to him while bringing him to the church?"

"No, I not talk to him. I just help him walk to here," the watchman said.

"Could you ask him in Sherbro or Mende his name and what he wants with us?"

"That not necessary, pastor. Me speak English too," Sengbe Pieh breathed.

Pen and the watchman edged themselves and stared at Sengbe Pieh.

"Me, I am Joseph Cinque. Africa here, me name Sengbe Pieh nor name Joseph Cinque," he said.

Pen still stood blank as if his biological clock had just been switched off.

"Me not understand. You be Joseph Cinque, the long long Sherbro for American slave?" the watchman stepped in.
Pen shoved him aside, "That's okay, Joe. Let me handle this."
Sengbe Pieh stared at the watchman and said, "Yes, me, and me come here to die in peace."
Pen urged the watchman to go back to his post. He then sat on the adjacent pew. The watchman reluctantly walked outside the church door. Pen thought for a while, and assured the old man that he was in the house of God where people were treated with respect. He suggested to him that he first needed to eat something if he was feeling hungry. Sengbe Pieh hurriedly accepted. Pen asked Sengbe Pieh to accompany him to his apartment. He then remembered that he himself had not even finished his food when he had heard the thumping at the gate.
Back at his residence, after they had shared a meal, Pen took out a bottle of red wine and surprised Sengbe Pieh with a smile. By this time, Pen had begun warming up to Sengbe Pieh. Pen poured a huge glass for Sengbe Pieh and a moderate one for himself.
Sengbe Pieh had a bushy mouth with his moustache considerably hanging over his lips. He parted the top moustache with his forefingers and took a big sip of his wine. He withdrew the glass, looked into it deeply and took a second sip of it. He breathed out deeply as if he had also taken a puff from a pipe. He was a smoker, but didn't feel that he should ask to be given anything to smoke after the warm welcome he had already received.
"What a young American you doing this part of me people's town alone?" Sengbe Pieh broke the silence.
"I am a missionary, a new missionary."
Pen wished he could instantly trust Sengbe Pieh the moment he disclosed he was Joseph Cinque, the man whose astronomical and historical image had moved him to opt to serve in Africa after graduating as a young clergy from Morehouse College. Since meeting Sengbe Pieh, Pen had fought very hard to restrain his

excitement.   Was it indeed true that he was meeting Joseph Cinque?

He was a child when the *Amistad* arrived in New York, and therefore, did not get to see the drama that resulted to the freedom of Sengbe Pieh and others of his countrymen.   Growing up in antebellum America, for Pen and many others, the achievement of the enslaved people of the *Amistad* was a heightened reality that the Black man could fight for and gain his freedom from slavery.

Since then, Pen had grown up with a badge of hot iron inside his chest.   He read voraciously and hungered after guts and glory during his college days.   Informed that as a free black man, the best opportunity for him to ever travel to Africa would be through the church, Pen decided to become a clergy.

"You wine, you not drinking you wine," Sengbe Pieh cut into Pen's thought.

Pen quickly fumbled with his glass, "Oh, I was just lost in thought..."

"About me, me know. Not you alone. Plenty people wonder too now, long time after me go search for me lost family."

"You lost your family?"

Sengbe Pieh instantly swallowed his throat.

"You lost your family in America or in Africa?"

"Lost family when went to slavery, see no family when me got back to Sherbro."

"Oh dear!"

"All me life me don look for family from Sherbro to Mende to Themne to the sea…but sea big, sea long."

An uneasy silence hung between them.

At once, Sengbe Pieh leaped from his seat and rushed to Pen, seized him by his cloak, "No, no, no, oh dear. Me nor give up on family, no, no, no. Me nor come here to die, me come to plead church to help me see me wife and children."   He became hysterical, pulling Pen's cloak off.

"You have to calm down old man, calm down!" Pen croaked.

"The church keep me family from me all these years...please don't be like them...tell me where the church took me family."

Pen continued to struggle with Sengbe Pieh to free his cloak from his grip. Sengbe Pieh was wailing at the top of his voice. Suddenly, the rain resumed more noisily than before. The door flew open as a heavy gust of wind entered the hall. Pen finally freed himself from Sengbe Pieh.

Sengbe Pieh he returned calmly to his seat as if to prepare for a final prayer. He appear broken as he searched for his glass, and raised it to his face. It was empty; nevertheless, he sipped from it and let it fall from his hand.

"You are drunk! I shouldn't have offered you more to drink. That's what it is...otherwise how can you accuse the church of stealing your family after all these years?" Pen shouted. "Have you come here for help or to accuse the church falsely about your missing family? In fact, how can anyone believe that you are indeed Joseph Cinque?"

Sengbe Pieh picked himself quietly from the pew and walked closer to Pen, "*Gbooooow* young pastor, how long you been here. Me sweat be here in this church. We fix the cross up in the arch and we open this place to local people, me people, to come to prayer to God. After America make me free, me turn back home, here after the good man, good old man, Jo...John Kinsi Adams and all him friends fight hard for we. Some people stay back, we say we come back home. Me come back for me family, me wife and three children. The church say they help find me family. Five missionaries come with us for open *Mende Mission*. We open *Mende Mission* and nobody look for me family. Pastor, me come from very, very, far place and me search for me wife."

He slumped to the floor and cried. In that moment, he carefully unwrapped from the bottom of his gown, a wrinkled rectangular piece of hard paper, which he handed over to Pen.

Pen took the cold paper and returned to his chair under the lamp. The paper was wet. He quickly realized that he was holding an engraving! He took a quick look at Sengbe Pieh who was still flung on the floor. The paper was dirty, and he could see nothing more that it showed. He put it aside on the table and returned to Sengbe Pieh.

Already Pen was moved by Sengbe Pieh's words. He bent over him to pick him from the floor to return him to the chair. Instead Pen looked into Sengbe Pieh's eyes and said, "Whoever you are, you have arrived in the place where God wants you to bring a closure to your search for your family or for anything you ever lacked. Please let me find you a place to sleep. The church has been searching for you since you left the *Mende Mission*. You certainly have a long story to tell me."

Pen returned to his chair, and for a while was lost in thoughts. The rain continued to pelt outside and a violent storm banged on doors and windows. As he leaned, his left hand nearly knocked down the lamp and the paper Sengbe Pieh had given him. He decided to take a keener look at it gain. He saw an unclear engraving on the paper. He began to make out the image of a man holding a staff. Below the image he saw written, *The Chief of the Amistad Captives*. He trembled, grabbed his glasses from his study, brought out a bigger lamp. He studied the paper more closely and thought he saw a young man leaping from it! Startled, he ran backwards and stumbled on Sengbe Pieh. Sengbe Pieh sprawled motionless across the floor! Pen heaved a big sigh and thought to himself, that after all, he was actually looking at the larger than life personality in the person of the old man sitting in front of him.

THE RAILWAY UNION

"**W**ho is this?" I demanded.

Silence.

"Hellooooo! Who is on the phone?" I breathed.

The shadows of slumber flickered off my eyes. I elbowed my pillow and brought my head to par with the headboard.

The belligerent caller thundered.

I listened, my face resting on the telephone handset. The pre-dawn silence sucked sweat off my body.

"You want to play the imitating game on me, eh? I see you want to play my game against me. You cannot even figure out what a union is, eh? Don't you know that a child who must wear his father's pants shall have his waist eaten by a rope? Now, if you don't stop the madness that I heard you and your union want to make, I will show you why monkeys don't eat pepper."

"Who is this?" I growled.

"You stupid and worthless boys!" the gravelly voice said, "That is what you are, right? I see that you cannot handle the Railway Union properly, eh?"

"Who is this?" My voice was beginning to crackle.

"Vistens! Pashaki Vistens!" the voice said. "You think you can create an impact out of this nonsense? Well, I have news for you! No two moments are ever quite the same in all of mankind's history. I got away with it then because the railway was the only hope of the people. I was fighting against everything colonial . . ."

My heart began pounding in its ribcage. I realized beyond any doubt that the chilling voice I was hearing was familiar.

The president's! The voice of the President of the Republic of Yugosoba!

It was foolish, but my first reaction was swelling pride at my sudden importance. The voice picked up again: "…everything! I fought against everything colonial in control of my people's lives!" Pashaki Vistens, the president of the Republic of Yugosoba continued shouting at me. "I didn't fight against my people or my people's leadership. My cause was genuine, and my struggle had nothing to do with money, sabotage, or that kind of thing. It was about a people's freedom. And that was all it was, nothing more. That moment has passed—it's gone forever. What you and your bunch of thugs are doing right now is nothing other than a civil disturbance. Believe it or not, none of you will get away with it!"

I heard the thunder of anger as the caller punctuated his threats by slamming his phone into its cradle. Suddenly nervous, I struggled to replace my own handset in the dark. What does it mean, I asked myself, when the highest authority of the land calls your bedroom phone on his private line? What would happen now?

I was the golden herdsman, president of the railway union. I rubbed elbows with people of power and wealth. Not being an errand boy, I was someone who had a kind of worth. I was someone others ran to for consultation. That was what I was: a worthy man; a man of the people. Over five hundred railway workers looked up to me for decisions affecting their lives: to work or not to work; to strike or not to strike; to accept or not to accept; to refuse or not to refuse. I determined them all.

But the herdsman too can be scared of the horns of his cattle. Stop them? I didn't know how to change the course of five hundred angry faces dripping hot blood, snarling with clenched fists, humbled only by the fulfilling realization of their own violence! They called it "spoiling the spoiler and the spoiled."

Imagine the audacity of authority!

Our union had a legitimate cause and the strike was our resolve. Salaries hadn't been paid in three months. On top of that, taxes piled up on the unpaid salaries.

One morning, we were directed to the notice board where we read that, retroactive to the first of several yet unpaid months, three new kinds of taxes would be added to the existing four. This revenue would enable our government to provide us with security, clean drinking water, and other needs at the dock. The union's interpretation of the new edict was that salaries were being drastically reduced to speed up the death of every railway worker and every member of his family. The government provided nothing for anyone, just unpaid salaries, which it regularly decreased with its senseless paperwork full of meaningless jargon. Fires smoldered in the hearts of the workers and anger overflowed the bounds of their souls.

The government's new tax notice came down that day in shreds. The next morning, a new notice went up, handwritten in italic style, probably by the minister of works himself. That one also, though spared shredding probably because of its calligraphic beauty, was torn down. A clerk in the minister's office passing by picked it up and reposted it on the board, perhaps innocently thinking it had been blown down by the wind.

For three more hours, the notice, now with big boot marks across it, hung on the board, before not just the notice, but the entire notice board, was brought down by some anonymous, angry hand.

The next day, , a notice, presented in a more official and impersonal font, was pasted on the bare wall with the swarning that the information on it had already been gazetted for national consumption and historical deposit. That, too, came down, and in its stead was boldly written:

The union favors the return
of the colonial masters.
They built the railway,
only they can manage it.

Until that sign went up, the ministry had treated the entire affair as union mischief. Now an offense had been committed, and it was time the union was made culpable.

Next, came the summons, from the minister. He wanted me at a meeting at 2:00 p.m. prompt the very day. The union quickly arranged a meeting of its executives to take place at the same time. I was expected to honor both meetings, an impracticable thing to do. Pressured by the union membership, I replied, with great humility, to the minister, telling him that I would be unable to personally attend his meeting in person under the circumstances. I offered to send three delegates in my place. If that was unacceptable, I asked him if he could kindly shift his meeting to another time of his convenience.

My response enraged the minister. He dispatched a letter disparaging my performance and reminding me that ". . . every citizen is bound to the service of the Yugosoba Government." He ordered me to call off all engagements that might conflict with his scheduled meeting, particularly those having anything to do with the union. Failure to do so would result in my suspension from my work and subjection to the laws of the land.

When I showed the letter to the union members, they hastily rescheduled our own meeting and whisked me away to it. I was shown a paper and told to sign. "Noted and desired," the paper read. That was my reply to the minister, composed by the union.

On national radio that day, the minister of broadcasting announced two resolutions: the government had banned the union; therefore, and its pending national strike was considered illegal. The next day, the minister of works fired off a letter to the union restating the resolutions. The letter was copied to the president, parliament, and the court of law.

The union fired back. Our letter reiterated our determination to proceed with the strike. That letter was copied to the Queen of Great Britain, her Prime Minister, the American Ambassador, president, parliament, the court of law, the press][(including the

BBC), the public, and whoever happened passed by the city's central cotton tree where the letter hung like a crucifix.

That evening, the national radio applauded the government's position, and berated the union for being childish and thinking that our letter would get any consideration outside of Yugosoba.

It was this madness President Vistens was referring to when he called me on the phone. Regardless of his outburst, I had always considered Vistens to be personally disinterested in affairs of this nature, and that he knew how to handle them with minimum of confusion for the benefit of everyone. In fact, I thought his involvement in the matter had merely been necessitated by the need for saving the skin of his minister—whom the independent press had blasted countless times as being politically immature. Every paper that came out that week accused the minister of blowing the incident out of proportion.

The president's threats could have spoiled my day, but I took comfort in the morning papers, which continued to support our action.

My home was no peaceful retreat from the affairs of the union. My two wives were always finding fault with each other, throwing the house into turmoil. Yes, I had two wives, but contrary to the belief of my friend, Konneh, I did not consider my marriages an act of polygamy. Where I came from, for a man to be considered a polygamist, he had to husband five or more wives, like my father did in his prime. He had six wives. In my village, a man who owned big and endless farms, like my father did, needed as many hands as he could get. Having multiple mates was the natural course of events. Very quickly, my father's six wives provided the farms with a huge staff of farm hands.

Nevertheless, my wives' boisterous and incessant hatred of each other continually proclaimed me a polygamist. If my father's six wives chose to argue at the top of their voices with each other at the same time, they would not equal the *gbomgbosoro*—the chaos caused by my two wives. The volume and intensity of their voices caused anyone approaching my household to think that I was married to several dozen women. Eight unruly children compounded the quarrel between my wives. Perhaps it was the uneven biological distribution of our offspring that caused the trouble among them: six to the elder wife and two to the younger. Sometimes, when the heat was too much and the house shook with feminine antagonism, I starved for weeks on end, plagued with various kinds of hunger.

That morning after the broadcast, I was confused about how to personally deal with the issue, especially now that it involved the president. I was by myself in my room all day, drinking palm wine and wondering what to make of the president's threatening telephone call. At first, I decided against disclosing the president's call to the union for fear that they would react foolishly, or to Konneh, my journalist friend, for fear that he would write all kinds of things about it. There are times, I believe, when a shepherd leads his sheep from the back. That was what I had done until the president's call. But now, I needed a smart confidante to help me work out the problem, so I sent my eldest son to invite Konneh to drink palm wine with me. After all, from previous interviews, Konneh already knew everything the union wanted or didn't want.

Presently I heard approaching footsteps.

"Some sober man is waiting outside to talk to you," Mabinty, my first wife said, peeking into my room. "Like always, he is here to make a man out of you. How can I ever thank the Lord for someone like him who is helping you open your eyes to see reason?"

"Who is it waiting for me?" I asked.

Ignoring my question, Mabinty walked away.

Of course, I knew at once to whom she was referring.

I met Konneh sitting in the living room. Konneh was the only man who had tried to stop me from marrying my second wife, and just for his effort, unsuccessful though it was, Mabinty held him in high esteem. When I crossed paths with Mabinty in the parlor again, I told her that Konneh had come to interview me for a biographical sketch to be published in his newspaper.

Although I didn't write too well, I hated anyone putting words on paper and asking me to claim authorship of them. I hoped Konneh wouldn't ask me to do that. We were childhood friends; we went to school together. He was the smarter, and I the stronger. We always argued about issues of brains and brawn. Toward the end of our teenage years we agreed that an endowment of both brains and brawn made one a genius, while an endowment of either of the two could make one a hero. He went on to the University of Yugosoba, and I made my way to the railway. By the time I was president of the union, he had risen through the ranks of journalism.

My success was measured by my title. Konneh's success was measured in numbers: three beatings (one leaving him with a broken ankle), five lock-ups (one that ran two years for libel against the son of a nephew of the spokesman of the first vice president's friend), and one award from the West, honoring fearless journalists in third world countries.

"What would you do with a threat like that from the president?" I asked him, after providing the details of my early morning telephone conversation.

"The question is for you to answer." He then asked, "What would *you* do?"

He took a big sip of his palm wine and waited for my answer.

"No. Don't play the interviewer tonight. You know I value your take on things like this," I insisted.

"Do you really? Oh, but of course I know you do, only you don't have the guts to think, even imagine, that you could do things my way," Konneh said.

"Our situations, you know, aren't quite the same."

"I don't understand what you mean by that," he said, puzzled by my remark.

"Like you, I have my life on the line in what I do," the fearless reporter explained.

"That is it!" I shouted. "You and I have our lives on the line, but maneuvering is obviously more difficult for me. You can simply sit there in that chair and singularly decide on how you want your writing to appear in tomorrow's issue of your newspaper, but I have hundreds of people to consult before I sanction any event or action."

"Very well, very well," Konneh said and held up his hands. "You are beginning to sound very much like them now," he picked up his glass and took a sip.

"Like whom?" I asked.

Konneh leaned forward in his chair and glared at me. "Like the ones you and I are supposed to be fighting against for what they are putting the country into," he practically spewed the words toward my face.

I shifted a little in my chair. "Perhaps I'm not fighting against anyone," I protested.

"Either way, you remind me of Vistens. Aren't you both presidents?" he asked.

"I will ignore that missile and spare you its response," I replied, reaching for my glass and laughing at his sarcasm. "Just answer my question."

He patiently finished his last few sips of wine, set the glass down, leaned back in his chair, and stared out across the room as he thought.

"What would I do, you want to know?" he finally said. "You know I'm not you, and you know what I'd do. I'd fire back."

"Look, this is no journalistic exchange to impress the public," I admonished. "And when it's over, I would still like to have every part of my body intact."

"Kandeh, can't you see you are in the wrong room?" He shook his head patiently. "You are lucky to have people around you who are interested in waking the dead person inside you. People read your name every day in the papers, yet they don't realize that you do not exist!"

"You think I'm dead?" I asked, charging from my chair with a new resolve. "Well I got news for you, Konneh. Vistens just knocked on my grave."

"Then I'll ask you this," he said. "When are you going to resurrect?"

I looked at him in the eyes and could tell that he was serious. I was inspired by his fearless personality and decided that for once, it would be fun to move against the gods of the country. I said almost in a whisper, "Have you got ink in your pen?"

"What colors do you want your name in?" asked Konneh.

"Build me a rainbow," I replied, and gulped my glass of palm wine.

"You just got one up in the sky," he said. "Just don't forget the light that burns behind it. Lazarus, walk forth!"

In that instant my wife, Mabinty, passed through the room like a polar sun that rises and sets in an instant. She fixed me with her gaze, but spoke to my best friend. "Konneh, do teach him how to be a man both at home and in the streets." She disappeared into the house.

"Is the war still raging between them?" Konneh, smiling, asked after Mabinty had disappeared.

For a moment, I felt the embrace of home and friendship blocking out the tension and trepidation my new resolve had stirred in me. "You tell me when it will end," I laughed and poured him another glass of wine.

"It'll end whenever you want it to end, Kandeh. Remember, a man in your position and with a political future such as the one ahead of you ought to set an example of being smart, right from the home."

"Are you saying our fathers were not smart when they married many wives?" I lowered my head and looked at him from beneath my brow. "I hope the ways of the white man have not settled too deeply into that head of yours."

Konneh waved his hand and shook his head in rebuttal. "Kandeh, don't confuse our days with the social lives of our forefathers, or even our fathers when they were in their prime. Many things that were socially accepted yesterday just cannot fit in today's society."

"Why not?" I asked.

We'd approached this theme many times from many angles. "Is it because the white man came and confused you? Tell me, what's the difference between the white man who has a wife and many concubines, and myself with only two wives and no concubine?"

Konneh took a sip of his wine before answering. "Now listen to this carefully. The difference between that white man—and I'll not even say a white man—the difference between the wise man with a wife and concubines, and you with two wives is that he keeps his troubles apart while you bring them together under one roof. You will never have peace in your home unless—and I must warn you, because your success with this railway struggle will depend on this—unless you resolve the situation under your roof."

My heart missed a beat, but I was not going to let Konneh achieve a victory on one issue by appealing to another. Draining my glass, I picked up the jug of palm wine and looked at it with mock seriousness. "If you're not going to stay on topic, then perhaps we should change the topic. I suggest the topic of palm wine," I said as I began to pour.

Konneh laughed aloud.

There ensued a conversation taking in all aspects of the palm wine we were sharing: its potency, flavor, color, and the merits of its effects on the spirit and on friendship. We finished the palm wine and had dinner.

Shortly afterwards, Konneh left.

I went to sleep thinking that the next day, being Saturday, would give me time to mull over all that had happened during the past few days. Although the railway operated on weekends, the union executives met only on weekdays, unless there was an emergency. As president of the union, I never worked on the dock. I spent all my time managing the union from a small office. I was told that Vistens had fought hard for that arrangement when he was head of the union. There had been twelve union leaders between him and me. I was the first union president to foment a crisis—as the president of the nation himself believed—by calling for a strike action. I'd had advice from many people regarding the upcoming strike, but I'd only discussed the telephone call with Mabinty and Konneh.

That Saturday morning, the house was left to Mabinty and I. Yeabu, my second wife, and the kids had gone to the market, because it was her turn to cook. I lay on my bed staring up at the ceiling and thinking about the turn of events. Mabinty came into the room and sat on the edge of the bed. She soothed my tormented mind with her words. I had told her that my heart was heavy about the strike. She wanted me to go ahead with it because the union was for it, and I would only get into trouble if I betrayed them. Of course, I was in favor of the strike, but with a telephone line across my throat, I didn't know how to handle the situation.

Mabinty climbed on top of me in the bed and began feeling for my heartbeat like a physician, all the time repeating that I need not be worried and that everything was going to be fine. I was about to express my doubts on the subject, but just then she slid her hand into my pants. We eyed each other and laughed.

Since I had married Yeabu a few years before, I had divided myself between the two of them three nights at a time. The truth was that I had long ago noticed how that marriage had considerably diminished the verve Mabinty once had. Now, there we were hot in the quickness of emotions and I was seeing a hint of her former self emerge. Yeabu had only begun her three nights with me, and, as per our household's understanding, Mabinty was supposed to have nothing to do with me sexually until her turn came about. The thought that the two wives were fire to each other did not elude me.

"I know how we used to be when it was just the two of us," I began.

"The thought, just the thought of you on top of her ...." Mabinty breathed.

"Don't start anything, Mabinty. You know it's not..."

She reached for my pants again more forcefully. I groaned in pleasure, shedding my hesitation. She had never done that before. I allowed both of us to luxuriate in the new sensation before finally pulling her up to me.

"Not that I'm objecting," I said. "But what brought that on?"

"I have to start doing the things that have made you love her more than you love me," Mabinty pouted.

"Do not think like that, Mabinty. You and Yeabu are two different people."

"Yes, I know how you think we are different. You think I am very, very old and she is very, very young. Try me."

She caressed me until I felt fire creeping through my flesh. Blood rushed into my head and my mouth watered for her. We hurriedly shed our clothes and went to it. I certainly hadn't planned this, and I don't think she had either. A thousand stars were popping inside my head when the door flew open, and Yeabu entered.

One wife had caught me having an affair with the other wife. Was that so bad?

No.

No?

Yeabu held the door wide open. We could hear the children approaching. I recovered from my shock and told her to shut the door. With a rage very much like that of a wounded lion, Yeabu released the door and entered, charging at us.

The door slammed shut behind her. She pushed Mabinty off me.

"You whore! Can't you wait for your turn?"

"What do you mean? Is he not my husband, too?" Mabinty hurriedly began to dress.

I went cold.

"Whose three nights are these? Can't you go sleeping with your dirty boyfriends in the meantime?"

"Who has boyfriends like you?" Mabinty retorted. "Besides, the turns were meant to be at night only. During the day either of us can have him."

Yeabu paused, but only briefly, as if she might buy that logic. "Do you always feel scratchy and cannot wait for your turn?" said my younger wife. "What is wrong with your womanhood? Are you a whore?" Her eyes burned with anger.

"It is you who are the whore, *obo!*" Mabinty shouted from the other side of my bed.

"Now tell me who is stealing the turn of her mate? Who? Tell me. You are a daylight thief, that's what you are!" Yeabu was now rudely clapping her hands.

"He is my man, too! He is not yours alone!"

"But you should wait for your turn, a thief like you. Don't we both have turns with him?" Yeabu shouted back.

I was thrown overboard with confusion. Although they had always fought like cats and dogs, Mabinty and Yeabu had never been this wild with each other. They'd now tripled the impact all my father's six wives would have made in their quarrels against each other at the same time.

To think that the argument had to do with sex! I was embarrassed, hoping our neighbors wouldn't hear them quarrelling. I scrambled out of the bed and began pulling on my clothes.

I must admit that it was very clear that I loved Yeabu more. I had only been married to Yeabu three years then, and she was ten years younger than Mabinty. I always looked forward to Yeabu's three nights. Before I married Yeabu, there were periods of three nights, four nights, even a week, when Mabinty and I did nothing in bed other than sleep.

Since my second marriage, if I only slept through my three nights with my first wife, she would cry and complain bitterly, hinting that Yeabu was sucking me dry. I always lied to her that I had also left Yeabu alone during her previous three nights, but she never believed me. For one thing, during Yeabu's three nights I went to bed early, while on Mabinty's nights I encouraged her to sit with me over palm wine discussing things of yesteryears until very late.

"Witch! Oh, you witch! You have bewitched Kandeh!" Mabinty shouted.

I choked with embarrassment. Peering through the window, I caught a glimpse of a neighbor's inquisitive face. I wanted to tell him that if he was so interested in my household, maybe he should stick his nose in my lavatory. Instead, realizing that the children were listening to every word, I redirected my anger to them. I opened the door and shouted at them to go to the back and not to sit in the parlor, eavesdropping on adult matters.

From over the fence of my compound came a burst of dirty laughter. More neighbors had been alerted. I held up a patriarchal hand and ordered my wives to stop, but I couldn't stop Yeabu, who was out-talking Mabinty. At first, Mabinty listened to my command. As usual, Yeabu was only infuriated by my voice. Mabinty could no longer restrain herself. Stretching like a snake, she grabbed Yeabu by her dress and pulled her to the ground. Then she reached for a chair and clubbed Yeabu on the head. She staggered and groaned at my feet. Stooping, she pushed Mabinty and registered three blows on her face.

Although blood ran from both their noses, I was the most helpless of the three, pained more by the dirty laughter of my neighbors, than by the foolishness of my wives. The first thought that came to my angry head was to shout out the window at my neighbors and threaten them by telling them that I could torment their lives with only one call to the office of the president if they didn't go away. That was foolish of me, but it was the thought that welled up in my angry and tormented mind.

I lost the opportunity that weekend to think about the matter of the union and the president's threatening phone call. In their anger, my wives shut the doors of their rooms against my face, and I was left sprawled on the living room floor, beaten down without having been touched by a single fist, and more confused than I had been in the morning.

During the night, however, I had time to talk with most of my executive colleagues on the phone. I told them about the call from President Vistens, but stopped short of telling them about his threats or the problem in my home. My colleagues suggested an emergency meeting with the membership the following day to address the issue before our strike.

That night I dreamed of President Vistens and his entourage visiting me at home. He and I embraced in the middle of my compound. He told me he knew the troubles involved in leading over five hundred unruly workers in a union like that of the railway. He offered me a deal. If I convinced the union to accept the proposed taxes, he promised to seat me in his political corridor and reward me at the appropriate time. He asked me to respond. For a while I lost myself in an imaginary political corridor where I found myself among giants who were already household names in the country. If I were seated in the president's corridor, I would be on my way to beating all odds and becoming a household name myself. I beheld the many eyes of the president's men, their broad smiles, exposing brilliant canine teeth. However, as soon as I began to address the president, the painful sting of a mosquito startled me from my sleep.

On Monday morning, without thinking about my unfinished dream or my wives' quarrel, I hopped in a taxi and went to meet my colleagues at the main station dock. As I approached, they broke into a victory song. Banners calling for the lifting of the ban on the union were mounted in the sky. I hadn't given a thought to the ban on the union, because I figured that if the president had called and talked to me about cooling the steam, the two sides were bound to reach a compromise despite his threat.

A long line of train coaches stood idly on the tracks. The trains that were supposed to have left that morning for the Marampa mines and the diamond town of Kono were motionless. After breaking off the song, the men informed me that the minister was the first to arrive at the facility that morning. He and his men had barred workers from entering the building. An hour had gone by before I arrived.

I was still trying to understand the situation when the minister stepped out of the building. Following close behind him were clerks and police officers. He carried a thick wad of papers that he carefully flipped through before raising his head to address me.

"Mr. Kandeh Kargbo, shouldn't you have announced your arrival here?" he asked.

"Oh, I don't usually do that, and besides, I'm just arriving. I'm surprised to see you here this morning, Mr. Minister, sir," I replied humbly, lowering my voice.

"Let's put it this way, I am going to be physically in charge of the docks for now," he informed me, adding, "I think matters have slipped out of your control."

Rumor had it that President Vistens had picked this loud-mouthed officer from the military and made him Minister of Works in order to control the union with a fist.

"We want to ensure," the minister continued, "that responsible railway workers are given the opportunity to serve their country.

We are not happy, of that these trains are standing here while innocent villagers are left miles away deprived of their rights."

I stepped away from the crowd and approached him. "But the union, sir, has…"

"Ah, yes! The union, did you say? The union is banned for now and you know that. I wish to deal with every one of you individually, but only as workers of the government," he said, moving away from me and talking to the crowd of workers. I realized at once that he had singled me out only to squeeze out any power that I might have left in me and to put fear into the hearts of the five hundred others, many of whom were illiterate. But I couldn't convince myself that my colleagues had been bought over or had suddenly lost their manhood.

He held up a loudspeaker and began to talk: "We have to ensure that this station is functioning again in the next hour. Workers are free to make individual choices, but whoever wants to return to work must sign a copy of the new government contract I am holding here. It states among other things that railway workers will remain loyal to the government and will individually be responsible for any of their actions. All those who wish to keep their jobs beginning the next hour must sign the new contract with the police officers in the booth across the tracks. Let me warn those of you who don't read and write that the main clause in the new contract also asks you to withdraw your membership from the union. I must add here that a more deserving union will later be constituted by government."

I turned to look at my partners. A deep silence wedged in their faces. Most of their banners had already fallen from the sky. Those who still dared to hold theirs up held them unsteadily. A few of the men, broken and disheartened, began to walk toward the other side of the tracks to sign the new contract.

My torment mixing with anger, I returned my eyes to the bright-faced minister.

"None of my members is going to look at your contract or sign it, Mr. Minister!" I barked, trying to keep even with his loudspeaker. A few grunts of support belched from behind me. When I turned to make an estimate, the number was encouraging; even those who had already moved toward the tracks paused. I knew I needed to push more to diminish the strength of the minister, just as he had attempted to diminish mine.

"Kandeh, are you aware of the sort of trouble into which you are leading these men and yourself? There is no reason to try to be what you can never be. You certainly cannot obstruct a government that must do its work," the minister growled.

His first mistake was, not talking to me through his loudspeaker.

"It's you who are obstructing justice, Mr. Minister," I said. "And like I told you, my colleagues won't even seek to understand your so-called contract. We wish to have an audience with a responsible official who will democratically address our grievances."

The minister swiftly turned to the police officers and whispered to them. I had seen his eyes widen at my use of the word "democratically," which the Vistens government had long ago redefined to suit their dictatorial tendencies.

"Your behavior is disrespectful to a senior government authority. At this hour, I order you to leave the premises of this station or else..."

"Not until your authority pays me my rightful due," I said, almost singing the words. "That money for which I have worked the past three months to provide for my family; even if it is only a tenth of your salary, it will make my family as happy as yours."

He paused, stupefied. I'd squeezed him by the balls! My colleagues roared in my support. The police surged. I stood my ground and continued to stare at the minister.

"You know Mr. Minister," I began. "Perhaps I should inform you that the president has offered to do the right thing," I lied.

"He has offered to discuss this matter with us. He called me up on the telephone."

"That would be in your dreams, Mr. Arrogant!" The minister bellowed. "I can see the publicity you want around you. A man must regard himself in the mirror before he thinks about moving a mountain. May I inform you that I have not come here for jokes and wishful thinking? Everything I do here is approved by my president."

His words were firm, but his voice was certainly less authoritative.

Suddenly, a man dashed from inside the office and whispered into the minister's ear. Doubt clouded the minister's face. He conferred briefly with the police then disappeared into the office. While we waited, my men released some of their tension with whispers of encouragement, urging each other to disobey the minister.

The morning had drifted into noon. The sun couched itself in the center of the sky. A large mass of clouds advanced like an army. The hills crouched in defensive silence as though they were all waiting for my command. At short intervals, union members came up to me and commended me for what they referred to as my "wisdom and bravery."

After some interminable minutes, a man in a dark suit appeared at the door and conferred with the police officers. My heart nearly stopped. I was familiar with police brutality. I had seen their efforts on the bare back of my friend, Konneh: the deep valleys of blood across his arms and the lacerations on his face. For the most part, I was not worried much about police brutality because there were only five of them at the meeting, all of them unarmed. I quickly sent a few of my men to comb the area to see if there were any snipers on the rooftops. They came back saying there were none. Finally, one police officer calmed the crowd, asking us to grant audience to the dark suited man.

"Gentlemen," he cleared his throat. "I will make this brief. The minister has just consulted with the State House, and regarding your grievances, he wishes the union to know that your executive members have been granted a presidential audience tomorrow at 2:00 p.m. Only your executive members shall attend that meeting, and—"

Whatever it was he said afterward didn't reach the crowd. How I found myself on the shoulders of two of my colleagues, I couldn't explain. The crowd broke into our victory song, marching out of the station with me in the air and replacing all the banners in the sky. On the roadsides, loitered the idle and destitute youth who displayed a perfect picture of the shame of the nation's economic adversity. I was noted for drawing government attention to this adversity.

Those destitute youth joined the crowd and heightened the refrain of my victory.

Our new victory and our jubilation in the streets kept a broad smile on my face during the day, but while I lay in bed at night, I wondered what would happen next.

Yeabu was all over me. Before getting up from bed, we made love with electric passion to make up for the nights of deprivation following what she called "cheating," which I called "jealousy." The following morning, I requested from my brew master a bigger jug of palm wine to charge my head and to develop my courage in lieu of the proposed meeting with the president, the feared bone breaker.

I sent my eldest son to invite Konneh to share my wine. While I waited for Konneh, I thought of all that had happened and was about to happen in my prophetic dreams. I had dreamed of a presidential visit to my house on one day, and the next day I would receive an invitation to go and meet the president.

My mind wandered.

Was I really going to be politically great? Was I going to be a minister and garner huge amounts of money and worldwide fame? Was I going to be great—great and fine?

To ensure that I said nothing to destroy my good fortune before the president, I wrote my speech carefully. Konneh was supposed to edit it, and I would caution him to divorce his radical views from my conservative ones, just in case he was tempted to shower my speech with his poisonous leftist ideas and obstruct my opportunity. I must confess that I feared Konneh's pen. It had led me into trouble many a time, but at the same time, I had great admiration for his insight.

I was beginning to wonder why my son was taking so long in bringing me back word from Konneh when I saw him, running breathlessly from Konneh's compound. I thought what a fine sprinter he was, although I hadn't tried to develop his talent. That little detail would be taken care of when I make it into the president's circle and was on my way to becoming rich and powerful. Wasn't my son himself fit to be sent abroad to be educated with state money for the benefit of the nation? We were going to see about the possibilities.

My son was still out of breath when he reached me. Exhausted, he managed to sputter that I should go into hiding at once. *What was wrong with him*, I wondered.

"You have to hide, Dad. Quickly! They are coming after you," he gasped.

"Coming after me? Who are? And what for?"

"They—they—they just murdered Uncle Konneh!"

"They just—what did you say?" My muscles tensed, and my head spun.

"I don't know—but there are some men out there—screaming for your blood, and—"

Without warning, the gates of my compound flew open. Plainclothesmen armed with guns invaded the pathways. Sporadic firing sent my family running for safety. What seemed like big bottles of fire went up in the air and landed on the roof of my house. I caught sight of my eldest son jumping over the fence. My wives and my other children were trapped inside the burning house. The rooms filled with black smoke.

I choked as I made my way into the house, cautious of the danger ahead of me but at the same time frantic to save my family. Three rooms yielded no sign of them. In the fourth, I felt someone on the edge of the bed. It was Yeabu. I carried her out of the room feeling for her pulse and was happy that she was alive. I breathed into her mouth, and she gasped. I hurriedly helped her through a window and followed, grabbing her beneath her arms and moving as quickly as possible away from the incredible heat and the people who'd started the fire.

From afar, I saw the house consumed by flames that reached into the night sky. The fence around the compound was completely broken telling me everything was destroyed. I hid in a derelict house. After the assailants left, I returned to continue the search for the rest of my family. All I remembered afterward was receiving a blow to my head that threw me to the ground unconscious.

When I opened my eyes later, I was in the company of my union executive members at the home of one of them. Apparently, a group of them had rescued my family and had found me unconscious. Still worried about the danger, they had divided my family into two groups between the households of two colleagues.

Yeabu and her two children and one of Mabinty's children were with me, while Mabinty and the rest of her children had been taken to another location. The decision was made to separate my family into two halves so that if the left hand of fate fell on any one half, the other might still survive to ensure that my family tree continued to grow.

Mabinty, I was told, had been reluctant to be the one separated from me. She had demanded to be with every one of her kids were fate to wrap its hand around her. She had been so uncompromising that my colleagues had to remind her that the kids she was making a fuss about were also mine, and that all my friends were doing was trying to save lives. It was obvious that they didn't read the truth in Mabinty's face.

I was angry and sad when I learned the reason for the attack that had cost Konneh his life. That morning, his newspaper had hit the stand with the interview he had done with me the previous day. My colleagues were able to secure copies of it before the ruthless forces of President Vistens stormed through the city beating vendors and readers who had it in their possession.

I was pictured on the front cover on the shoulders of two men with an inset of President Vistens on the left and a bold headline underneath that read:

TWO PRESIDENTS IN A HOT CONTEST

Konneh had written:

For the first time in the history of post-colonial Yugosoba, democracy is poised to be tested to the benefit of all black Africa. The single-party government of President Vistens has been challenged on the principles of good governance, justice, and the culture of genuine representation by the most powerful pressure group in the country, the Railway Workers' Union.

This unprecedented chapter in our nation's history threatens to expose the abuse of power in government departments, the yellow cry of the helpless poor constantly brutalized by a government they voted in power.

Many years ago, President Vistens was born by the oars of unionism to topple the government of Prime Minister Magran. He had lured the nation into a trap and had subjugated democracy by announcing a single-party system of government.

In the afternoon, word came to us that the general membership of the union had defied my plea to stay action. About four hundred men took to the street protesting everything, from the killing of Konneh to questions about the legitimacy of the Vistens government. An hour later, the crowd grew to thousands. The government responded by sending its military after the crowds. The city was nearly brought to its knees, blood sprinkling everywhere. Following the funereal silence after the guns, government declared a dusk to dawn curfew a few hours later. The national radio blamed the disturbance on the union one thousand times over. That evening, the president was on the radio for what seemed like forever.

"Fellow countrymen," he began his broadcast, "This is your president talking to you with a heavy heart. We had awakened from sleep this morning with every expectation we would live happily through today just like we have always done under the protection of my government. We were never aware that we had among us satanic enemies born from the womb of hell. They decided today to turn our beloved country into a war zone. These men engaged our security forces in combat without regard to the innocent lives around us. We are grateful to our ever-loyal forces which have captured these men and taken them into custody.

"My government will interpret the laws of the land to bring them to justice. While a few of them remain in hiding, my government is searching for the leading criminal, the notorious and unpatriotic Kandeh Kargbo. I entreat you all as good citizens to assist the law enforcement officers in tracking down and stopping these dangerous men.

"Let me read you a note I received from the membership of the railway workers appealing on behalf of the larger body of the union who never supported Kandeh Kargbo and his small group of thugs.

"The note says, *It is sad when men who cannot control their own homes undertake to lead the public lives of other men. Very soon they destroy all the values of the society. This is exactly what Kandeh Kargbo, the self-styled leader of the railway union, has done. Kargbo, a man with six wives and countless number of children, is corrupt, inept, and dangerous. He has embezzled union funds since forcing himself upon us. He slept under a roof which he had very little control over; all he was interested in doing was taking a new wife every year.*

"*The members of his household always fought with each other and have terrorized the entire neighborhood. Kargbo constantly threatened helpless parents to turn over their teenage daughters to him. Sometimes he used force to own these innocent girls whom he kept as sex slaves. We workers of the railway are calling on every Yugosobian to rally behind President Vistens. He not only provided the railway with exemplary leadership during his time as a railway worker and leader of the union, but also he is currently serving the nation better than any leader this nation has ever had.'*

"Fellow Yugosobians, this letter was given to me by the law-abiding citizens working at the railway. Furthermore, my government has deliberated the liabilities involved in running the age-old railway station. Last year alone, my government invested eighteen million Leones in the railway, and what was its income? It was only a total of seven million. For the past five years, each year has been worse than the year before it.

"We are aware of the mass manufacturing of motor cars, trucks, and buses in Europe and other places. My government has held consultations with all the wings of government, traditional chiefs, and you the voters, as to the viability of keeping and running these colonial trains. As a democracy, we have listened to your responses that it is not profitable to keep a broken system running. Therefore, fellow citizens, over the next six months, we will begin to phase the railway out of service in this country. This exercise will end in less than one year. The country shall enjoy a constant supply of private and public vehicular transportation from Britain and Japan..."

And for the rest of that evening, Vistens droned on. Tears filled my eyes. I mourned Konneh. I mourned Yugosoba. I mourned my own life.

THE MIRROR HAS NO MEMORY

I had two concerns as I stepped out my door at 8:30 that morning to visit her at her home. I wondered if she would ask me just to lie face up in the bed, while she elicited pleasure from my body as she always insisted, and whether she would also demand that I stay with her all day in the green lagoon of her lust while her husband was busy establishing himself in the new Republic of Chaos?

Both prospects raced my heart.

For one thing, whenever Mrs. Gimi More entangled me in her being, she pulled, and tore all over me with such violence that I ended up a victim of her desire. In those moments, she was a woman ridding herself of a pain put in her body long ago by someone who was supposed to be her *real* man.

Mrs. Gimi More starved me with no food all day. She used the flimsy excuse that going in and out of the room would alert her neighbors, who often came to her doorsteps asking for a mortar and a pestle to pound their yams, or for leaves and salt for their broths, as if she was the epitome of domesticity. Besides, she would say, what about the prospect of someone discovering me in her bedroom?

In my unpredictable anger, I had tried to warn her that by not providing me food to eat in the interim of lovemaking, my guts would be in such pain that I would be unable to continue making love to her. Since she never paid any attention to my complaints, before I honored her nagging invitations I learned to get my fill with the cheap food sold at a local slum cookery stall with the allowances she gave me. If the truth was to be known, I also visited the stall because it was a center for people's gossip—a local information center.

The Mammy Felleh Cookery Shop leaned considerably to one side with age and neglect until all the zinc ripped into shreds. The Harmattan wind beat a perpetual noise out of the structure, causing customers to shout their orders so they could be heard.

"Do ya, mek ar get rice with cassava leaves!" was regularly re-echoed by three or four customers before the large Mammy Felleh or one of her two aides responded.

Conversations of many kinds popped up along the counter from the people waiting to have their orders filled. There was talk of credits and debits, of household disputes, of lovers, friends and foes, of sports and athletics. There were stories about the good old days and hard times. Eventually, all the talk drifted to a common topic: the sorrow brought about by the war.

Ours were the longest lunch breaks I had ever had. We were the unemployed and ne'er-do-wells. Our judicial structure had a loaded agenda of state matters. Most pervasive was the corruption of elected officials and other public hangers-on, not fit (according to collective opinion) to run the country. However, this was gossip that I did not like to be a party to. Someone would eventually pick a topic that was directly related to me while I sat there, unable to say a thing in response. Just as I had feared, someone had always mentioned Gig.

I did not like to talk about Gig and the vigilante group in public. I was a part of this vigilante that Gig headed, the only militia that the government and the police recognized as having a legitimate right to patrol greater Freetown in the townships of Waterloo, Tombo, Hastings, Funkia, and Adonkia in this time of war. This assignment was created after the guerilla rebels who'd been fighting the government for the past four years in the hinterlands sent a letter to the government saying that they were ready to attack Freetown. The government needed a militia group to help the military in guarding the city.

It took ten minutes to get the 'rice and cassava leaves' that I had ordered. I always requested a large brass spoon that allowed me to scoop more than the usual silver spoon did. I believe I was the only university graduate with first class honors visiting that place. Had I succeeded in my last interview, which I had attended, dressed with a tie and a waistcoat, I could have bid farewell to Mammy Felleh's cheap BLD: Breakfast, Lunch, and Dinner.

Again, like my previous interviews, Mrs Gimi More had put in a word, to the wrong person, at the wrong time. A former college mate of mine, who happened to have been a relative of Mrs. Gimi More's contact person, won the job, regardless of his third-class degree and lack of experience. How did I come to know that? I ran into him one lunch hour. He was dressed in a necktie and waistcoat, and he was headed for GEM, an expensive Lebanese-owned tourist restaurant, for lunch. He told me of his impressive job role to a job, for which I had applied but failed, as he entered into GEM's air-conditioned interior. I was left standing in front of the restaurant's tinted glass door. Dumbfounded. It was the nearest I had been to GEM. As I stood outside trying to look in, the tinted windows reflected my disheveled sweat-soaked image. Quickly, I tucked my shirt into my trousers and put myself together in a manner befitting a university product who, even in times of economic depression, must remain a vanguard of positive allusion. Without regard to my presence, the glass door rudely flew open, flinging my image aside, as though some secret arbiter of social standards had pulled it away from the restaurant.

From the open door, there issued a small knot of wild, attractive young girls, the sort that I had always dreamed of having in bed instead of Mrs. Gimi More.

Suddenly, The Mammy Felleh Cookery Shop erupted with noise. Every chair filled, tables were crammed with food and drinks, aisles bustled with customers. People streamed in through the front and side doors. Some of us who had finished our meals delayed our exit from the facility for the obvious reason of being idle. Others ordered more food. A stench hung in the air due to overcrowding The zinc structure like the people it housed was wet, and so was the floor. Once again, the crowd cried out, *"kasadalif!"* followed by the loud clanking of plates and spoons and the scorching call for *"wata!"* to drink. Responding to the cries, a child sauntered through the crowd with a container, and announced the cost per polythene.

In addition, two other children added to the refrain, *"Cold Ice!"* The redundant phrase informed buyers that it was not just cold water they had: they were selling unthawed ice; therefore, it came with a higher price. Opposite where I sat were two big fellows, who were known for calling out for service every other hour. Currently, they sat over their empty plates talking loudly to each other. The crowd was drawn to a large number into listening or contributing to it. I was one of those. And in my idleness, I remembered Mrs. Gimi More. Each time Mrs. Gimi More crossed my mind with her passion for wild sex, my desire for reordering lunch grew. Food soon became a weapon to subdue eroticism.

"Did you guys hear that Gig has ordered the stadium officials to cancel all soccer matches?" one of the big fellows asked. He was known as Extro, short for extrovert. His partner was Intro, short for introvert. Those who knew them well did not need to be reminded that the pair hated those names like hell. One felt tarnished by the sobriquet; the other felt affronted.

"And who is this Gig to cancel a soccer match just like that? Has he got anything against the sport?" said a frail man, licking his spoon like a starving dog, and straining his neck to closely observe Extro and Intro. Extro turned to look in his direction. He might have slapped the frail man if he had been closer.

"What are you talking about? Do you know who Gig is?" Extro grunted.

"I know he is not a sports official, to say the least," the frail man replied. "Otherwise…"

"Otherwise? Otherwise what?" Extro said..

The frail man did not like Extro's demented look. He shifted his empty plate before him and belched so hard that the crowd burst out into laughter. Extro felt better.

"The Eagles football team cannot come for the match because the rebels have blocked the Freetown-Kono highway," Extro continued from where the frail man had interrupted him, looking around to make sure we all made sense of what he was saying.

"So, you are saying Gig warned match officials that the Kono team wouldn't come to Freetown because of the rebel roadblock?" said the frail man, undaunted. Intro, who had not said anything until then, shouted him down. But the frail man persisted. "It couldn't have been Gig who cancelled the soccer match," he said.

"Then, who did?" asked Intro.

"Only the government has such powers," said the frail man.

Two or three other people who had merely been listening to the exchange now chimed in to tell the frail man he was being a nuisance. Intro then went on to tell him who Gig was, just in case the frail man had suddenly materialized from God-knows-where. He told the man that a vigilante commander like Gig sat in every security and social committee, sometimes even as chairman or secretary. We began to wonder what this frail man was really interested in anyway. Was it the cancelled soccer match or Gig? Who was he by the way? Was he a rebel spy among us? Everyone wanted to know.

During the war, to be branded a rebel in the city of Freetown was to be made a prey to mob justice. There was the story of a boy who snatched a purse from a helpless woman in a crowded marketplace. The chase took the two of them into meandering streets, but only the woman worked up a sweat. She began losing her attacker until she had the sense to shout, "Rebel! Rebel!" Almost automatically, the entire street took chase. The boy, aware of the stake and the furnace awaiting his apprehension, protested.

"I'm a thief, not a rebel!" he cried. "I am a thief, not a rebel! I stole her purse. Here it is!"

"If you don't know, Gig has his eyes everywhere," said Intro, who still had the floor. "Just turn your oversized head and see who is watching over your thick skull." Intro spoke not to threaten, but to caution.

I was not surprised. Anyone could identify me. Every vigilante member was nearly as well-known as Gig himself. I was embarrassed that with all my education I should be associated with the abstract nature of violence, so that the frail man had to always be on his guard, fearful of speaking his mind. The consensus was that I could either physically humble him or pass a command to achieve the same.

The poor man turned and grinned into my face. I quickly turned away.

"You want to be a big mouth? Badamaci will teach you a lesson," Extro growled.

"All right, all right," the frail man said.

It was my turn to inquire of these bullies who happened to know my name. Why hadn't I left after I'd had lunch? Everyone's concentration shifted from the frail man to me. Had I quickly responded to Mrs. Gimi More's invitation after eating, I would have been saved from the embarrassment of this moment. I was always proud to be identified as one of Gig's henchmen. I felt elated to be considered in the company of his closest boys: Kabila, Shaka Zulu, and Fidel Castro, boys who had almost lost their real names in the inferno of the war. They were so popular by their adopted names that I thought of getting one myself, like Winston Churchill. I would then keep Badamaci for use in purely academic circles, and, yes, for the comfort of Mrs. Gimi Moore, who thought my name meant a Bad Man with No Mercy.

However, she only told me so whenever I turned down her invitation for sex. But when she was feeling horny, she would say, "Do you know what your name stands for? Do you?" She would breathe hard into her telephone and almost grunting, she would answer her own question. "Your name stands for Bad Man—Have Mercy—on a starving woman who cannot run around like your little girls. That's it. That's what your name stands for, loving darling. Are you going to come?"

"I'll only stop by…I'm not myself today," I usually replied.

"You're going to be just fine, just fine. You just stop by for a while."

"*Bro,*" someone in the crowd addressed Extro with ghetto respect. "Is the match really cancelled? I cannot wait to see the Eagles' defense in the field of play. To get past that defense with a ball is like breaking through a wall. The boys have the wall. You can't just shoot past them all; no matter how hard you dribble the ball."

"You must be talking history," Extro began. "That was before, when the Eagles had a player like Koboko as their main back. Ever since he got scrapped in their last match with the Lions, their defense tumbled down like the great Berlin wall. However, making up for that loss is the strength of their center forward. *Ooh!* They have the best center forward I know. No need for their defense to sweat."

"Super, for the best center forward, you are surely looking in the wrong direction." Intro, who supported another team, begged to differ with his partner.

"Let's hear what you have on your list," Extro taunted as if whispering to someone, but he spoke loud enough to be heard on the town square. He said, "Now let's hear what Fisheries can do. I know that's your team."

"You want to know the truth?" asked Intro.

"Well, let's hear the truth according to the Fisheries team supporter," Extro responded.

"The truth is that every good spectator knows that the Fisheries team has the best center forward set up today, and not just because I'm a fan," Intro countered. He obviously had considerable support from the audience.

The soccer subject brought a friendly disposition to the crowd, eliminating every tension and fear. Players individually came under scrutiny with solid analyses of their performances as well as goals they had scored and number of appearances made. There was talk of the international trading of players. A disagreement about who was the most expensive Sierra Leonean soccer player divided the crowd. Even though Extro insisted on a particular player, his choice did not make the first five in the arguable best. For one thing, there were no reliable statistics to support anyone's claim. Someone cautioned that no one should trust the figures appearing in the local dailies: how could reporters, who had never obtained visas to a European country, know about the contractual fees of overseas players? Add this to the fact that the players themselves do not usually want their earnings disclosed to the public, and then you get a better understanding of the journalistic farce in this country today.

Another voice dismissed all the comments as rubbish. "What with the explosion of the Internet," he said, "the local teams that originally owned the traded players always know about such contracts, and they feel proud about publishing the financial worth of their players to attract new talents to their clubs."

"You get Internet? You know Internet?" asked a rather mucky voice that could not be fitted to a face.

"This stupid war raging over our heads is depriving us of good soccer," said the frail man, again bursting with anxiety. "How is this country supposed to discover new talents? This useless war has not allowed us to see a professional soccer match in a long time. Now look at the stadium lying dormant. Morale is down, and every good player is going abroad. Today, there are more Sierra Leonean players in one foreign team than in any one team in the country."

The frail man earned himself some respect again with his outburst, which received a standing ovation. He talked about the state of world football, comparing it to other sports, like basketball and how the latter was thriving well in the United States.

From deep within the crowd, the mucky voice came up again. *"You dɔn go de? You know America?"*

This question provoked a brief laughter before the silence returned. Resuming, the frail man said that because the United States did not show much interest in what he called "international soccer" and was not financing it, the football World Council, FIFA, was finding it difficult to promote the sport the way it should be.

Another man in the crowd took the reference to the United States as an opportunity to veer off on a tangent. "The United States never honors its debt owed to the UN because it wants the UN destroyed," the man said.

A towering figure nearby jumped in. "Do you think that America is incapable of paying its debts? America is the richest and most powerful country in the world," he literally shouted out.

Another voice cried, "Why then won't America pay its debts, if it is so powerful?"

The crowd disagreed for a while about America being a shallow bigmouth and a country trying to boss the rest of the world around.

"It is not called America; it is called the United States of America," the mucky voice shouted again.

Another feat of laughter followed.

"What's the difference?" the previous speaker questioned.

Looking around, Extro came down heavily on the man's leg like a wrestler, reminding the others they were not there to discuss America or the United States of America, or for that matter *Amerigo*, or whatever it was called; they were there just to discuss football. He urged the frail man to continue his explanation.

As if to prevent further trouble, the frail man shifted his focus to Brazil. He spoke for five minutes about Pele, whom he called by his little-known original name, Edson Arantes do Nascimento, and particularly about his recent role as a politician in the sports affairs of his country. He then turned to Europe where, he said, "Football rests its head on fine pillows."

He spoke about why hooliganism in football matches was as European as a cup of tea. Regarding the many African football stars going off to play for European teams, he said it was an African reversal of power base. In other words, it was African colonialism of the West. He then went on to establish an unclear theory of why black people were excelling in sports more than any other race. Then he rested his case. He had successfully stolen the show from the big fellows, who had little to say about international football.

Everyone agreed the war had destroyed most of Sierra Leone's institutions. The war had been raging for four years now. People seemed to be slithering like snakes on smooth surfaces, with a conspicuous inability to forge ahead. When the war first broke out, people were still attending football matches, but with guns all over the place, players and spectators were shot, football officials lost their money, and the whole institution was stuck rotating on an undecided trust.

It occurred to me that the football and war situations were like the one between Mrs. Gimi More and I. There had never been a relationship *per se*, at least as far as I knew it. I enjoyed the union, but it was she who did all the groaning. There were times I looked in the mirror and said to myself, "Badamaci, sex is a gainless labor." Then for a while, I resisted every temptation that came my way. However, after a few days of celibacy, I missed her and began to smolder with a fresh fire. I was like a starved spectator, wishing for a good match.

For me, sex had become not just an appetite that lingered on among young men of my generation, but a survival skill. During the war, brothels were converted into royal houses with young peasants like me rising to kiss the lips of princesses. In war, as in soccer, people talk about attack, defense, retreat, and advance. No matter how you looked at it, sex was a type of war, and all I came away from the university with was the instinct to survive on it. With an old hand like Mrs. Gimi More, I was caught up like a graduate of books.

In our war, single women became Miss-Hard-to-Get, or was it Miss-Hard-to-Meet? These girls, mostly in the hands of men in authority, are warming the beds while their wives find refuge in unexpected places. The starving lots were married women. At night they littered the streets in the nude, under the pretext of saving their children from running off to become guerilla combatants, but they ended up in the embrace of men the age of their children. Mrs. Gimi More often told me she missed the vigor of my youth lost in her husband without dreaming of growing gray. When I listened to her groaning on top of me, she told me how her husband was busy creating a place for himself in the larger republic, I could not help thinking how our war of polychromatic anger was all about failed relationships.

It wasn't Gig who had brought me into the vigilante movement. I had been dribbled as a ball. Originally, I had opted for the military, now stretched. Resources were low. The government needed more recruits than it needed officers. In addition, the reality was that the government was at ease recruiting children whom they paid nothing. As one government official told me, adding that it was for my ears only, "We are sending the equals of our enemy's child soldiers to war. On the other side, they have children who march into war with no reservations. Our adult soldiers have their wives to think about. Many of them have perished at the hands of children. The children we send to war are our only saviors."

In my case, the official advised me to linger in the government-approved vigilante group, waiting for the end of what he called, "this recklessness." A note to Gig made it possible.

Gig had taken a liking to me at once. He always took me around with him, making me draft reports and write correspondences for him to sign. Some weekends he invited me to drink beer at his place. A vigilante may be a volunteer, but I was never a soldier in reserve. I did not have to be on the front line of the war front, although I carried a licensed weapon along the streets in my neighborhood by day and by night.

We ignited bonfires in the compound of those we protected, sang songs of bravery, activities that were enhanced by guns, alcohol, and marijuana. One day an angry old woman said to me, "You boys are doing well by protecting us, but to sing into our ears in the dead of night is to have us carry the war into our meager sleep. God save us!" Immediately, I thought she was being ungrateful. I looked into her eyes with the anger of a completely dry spirit and spelled W-A-R backwards for her. I told her that was what we were. Moreover, I added, "God save the Queen and her husband. God save the monarchy. God save colonialism, post-colonialism, and anti-colonialism. God save the military and God save the military's alter-ego, the vigilantes. God save the perpetrator. God save the victim. God save other gods."

I meant to make her look irrelevant. She stared me in the face with the bitter aspect of elderly conceit and said she wished she could trade places with the dead. When I offered to help her achieve her wish, she cried like a baby.

The community complained about me to Gig. Gig visited our camp, and with one long look at me, he decided I had what it took to lead a unit. He told me that he wanted to put some sense into my head for that new role. I told him I already had enough of it with honors I had received from the university. He tapped me on my back and said it was a shame that my country could not find a dignified place for me, with all my learning.

"It's all right," I told him. "All of us are displaced anyway."

Gig was a man with a soaring ambition. Once he told me his dreams were complex even for his own comprehension. He liked to talk late into the night. He never drank alcohol, but he was addicted to coffee. Gig did not believe himself to be a soldier. The weight of an AK 47 on his back made him stoop. He shook like a reed when a cold wind blew. He was always scared when, for instance, a tire burst into flames. These have happened a few times. Moreover, the thought of war unnerved him. In fear, the first thought that came to him was of his family: his wife, first and then his only child, whom he had managed to send to his sister in England. Whenever he was leaving a place, he always remembered to pick up his mug but forgot his gun, even if it was lying right in front of him. A few weeks later, he paid the ultimate price for that habit. Gig had great potential. He thought himself a diamond because as a young man, he was aware of his potential. He had always wanted the best for a country that had gained independence at the same time as he had. His father had told him on his twentieth birthday that he was a grown man, and therefore was free to go out into the heart of the country by himself. "Now that the British have given us a breathing space to properly own our country," his father had said. Heeding his father's advice, Gig had gone and kept going into the heart of the country. He told me that maybe, at mid-life; he had gone too deep or too blindly to be of any more use to himself.

"I'm always troubled by my fratricidal compatriots whom we have made into leaders," he said. "When our freedom-founding fathers wanted the British to go, they complained a lot about the injustices of colonialism and the enslavement of the black mind. No sooner were they in control than they began nurturing violence toward each other."

He paused and sipped heavily from his coffee. "Every young man then needed a role model," he said. "We looked up to those of our elders who, during the white man's rule, had gone abroad and educated themselves. But when they returned, they fell below our expectations and allowed their differences to manipulate them. When I look back, I pity their blindness to the historical significance of their era. In their foolishness, they inflicted wounds in our hearts."

He buried his head for a while and when he raised it, his eyes were as red as the setting sun. "I have a duty to turn this system around for young minds like yours."

The war had taken considerable energy from Gig. He depended on his stoicism, along with what little substance was left in him, to run the affairs of the vigilantes. That night was the closest I ever came to him. Although he threw his power all over the place, it was his stoic ghost that did all the talking. Thereafter, it was not unusual for the two of us to sit down away from the bonfire with the night spell off our brows and talk about the ways of the world. A tire exploding in the furnace made him to jump, splattering coffee all over himself. He whispered his wife's name and that of his child. He drank heavily from his mug with a nervous hand.

"I came into this to save my country, but already my own life is pushing too hard on me," Gig said, almost in solitary conversation with his mug. "I know the rebels will attempt to come to Freetown. I must warn you, Badamaci." He turned to me and said, "Watch yourself, and watch your neighbor. In times like these, a man reaps what he sows. The government does not trust the national army any longer. There have been too many renegade soldiers, more than enough to start a platoon. Watch yourself, if you want to grow old. I am doing this for my family. I love my wife a great deal, but I notice the war has taken a lot of her from me."

He turned towards me again, and after a moment I realized that he was staring intently, eyeing me longer than he ever had, almost as though he wanted to stab my eyes. I remained silent. "After all this madness," he continued, "I will go into forests, mountains, and rivers to rescue her." He paused and took a heavy sip of his coffee. I could hear his throat gulping. "Badamaci, do you make love to a woman with a complete forgetfulness of any state of affair?"

The question did not sink into me properly, but I grunted. He took that as an answer, but I did not know whether he had taken it as a "yes" or a "no." I waited until he removed his flask from his knapsack, refilled his mug, took a sip, and threw his gaze, perhaps his very mind, into the fire.

"Did you just ask whether I make love with . . .?"

"Never mind," he waved a hand. "If you had made love during your university days and still came out with first-class honors while your colleagues sweated their asses over their books for nothing, what other state of affairs, especially one during a war time like this, could matter to you? Maybe one theory you might like to expand on in your future learning is that the best time to make love to a woman is during moments of tension, when every pain has been achieved. You exploit her feminine vulnerability.

"Think of all the wars you have read about," he said. The world wars, Napoleonic wars, Hitler's war, the Burma war in which Sierra Leoneans fought. The other day I was talking with old Corporal Kargbo, who himself fought in the Burma war. I wanted him to help us manage the vigilantes, but all that was in his head was the memory of the young Asian girls he made love to by the dozens. Do you know that pain prolongs a man's pleasure?

"Every brutal act, whether by soldiers or rebels, has been interspersed with romance, and the reverse is not always the case. In civilian terms, the fighter's romance is only known as rape. I have heard of rebels raping corpses. There was a rebel who was so touched by the beauty of a corpse he chanced upon in the nude; he carried her on his shoulder fifteen miles and hid her in a derelict house. It is alleged that he made love to her every other hour. After a while, he declared to his colleagues that he had discovered the African Nomoli whose beauty outclassed the Italian Madonna. Well, of course he didn't mention the Italian

Madonna by name, but when he said, 'more beautiful than all of God's creation' he meant the Italian Madonna, Beersheba, every Egyptian queen, Nefertiti, Marilyn Monroe, and Romeo's Juliet. He told his squad mates that she was a fresh corpse with the silence of one who will be resurrected after every painful fandango. One day after the sun had fallen behind the huge black hills, he shut her up in the house, protecting the only door and window with stones and trees. He urged his colleagues to do the right thing. *He* was going on the road. He would be the urgent revolutionary, and in so doing, would save the only known Nomoli. She was destined to be resurrected at the end of the war to produce new virgins and romantic saints, who would in turn make the world a better place. Marching like a Neanderthal, the rebel went into the hottest part of the battle and was never heard from again."

I hiccupped when I did not hear the young man talk again. The bonfire was dimming a few meters away. In the darkness, he sipped heavily at his coffee. I wanted to ask him many questions, but I could not break his silence. I wanted to know what happened to the African Nomoli. What kind of spirit took possession of the young man? Why would he mess with a dead woman? It was as though Gig read my thoughts.

"The woman was not dead, she was only a corpse," he whispered but I was not what to make of that statement. It certainly was very loaded as was the thought inside him. He sounded heavier in this single utterance than he had in his entire disturbing story. I wanted to tell him how much he was torturing my mind, but when I looked away from the fire, he had gone into the night. I shamefully acknowledged that Gig had indeed put a lot of sense into my University head.

The next day I entered the Mammy Felleh Cookery Shop only to find it cold and silent. Only three people sat at the counter: two at one end, and a lonely man sat near the door. Nobody was eating, although it was way into lunchtime. One thing I knew, because I ate there every day, was that something was not right for the Mammy Felleh Cookery Shop to be so cold and silent at a time like that. I began to wonder whether Mammy Felleh had fallen ill. But I would have heard about her from the people I met.

My mind went back to the last accusation she suffered in the local dailies. It was alleged she ground dried goat shit on the hard skin of a seashell and washed it with the ink of Quranic surahs on a tablet and cooked it in her potof broth to attract customers. The report had threatened her business, but after she tactfully began advertising on television, the crowd had gradually returned and eventually grown to such overwhelming proportions as she had never seen before.

It was that prodigal crowd of customers that had brought along the two big fellows and the frail man. Nobody knew where they had come from, and everyone knew they were not from our community. However, they soon became known and respected in their different ways. None of them was a member of the vigilante movement, and I was surprised that these two robust men were not part of our group. Although the two big fellows were known to be boisterous, all they argued about was soccer. Extro had fought on two occasions with people who had dared to openly disagree with him. The good beatings he had given them had sent ripples into the spine of everyone. The frail man became known as Socrates, because he always had something strange to say about faraway places.

I saw Mammy Felleh coming out of her kitchen.

"What's the matter? Mammy Felleh, have you run out of food?" I asked.

"No," she answered, "I have run out of customers. What is it about soccer that is making you men crazy?" She examined her lunch bowls.

"My answer, Mammy Felleh, is I want to eat a very good food before any football player comes here."

We both laughed.

"Well, it seems they are really going to play football here today and if they are so worked out, my food will sell well."

"How is that? How come!" I asked.

"You have not heard? You are the only one I know who doesn't have the fever."

"Why? I heard that lunch is ready, and I'm starving and down with the flu."

"If you haven't heard, the Eagles are going to turn the city upside down today. You'd better braced yourself for the match."

"The Eagles are coming down to Freetown! I can't believe this."

"You better do. I understand that Gig gave the okay last night to the sports officials, and come to think about it, you should know about that. It has been arranged that the Kono team will come to Freetown today. You can see this place is empty because everyone is on the highway to welcome the team."

Just then the distant shout of exuberance drifted in with the wind, reverberating like the passion of the ocean tide crashing on concave banks.

"That," Mammy Felleh said, hesitating, "is too loud for a soccer match."

"Only, if we don't win. I hope the scores are good for us," I said as I moved off to the direction of the noise.

When I stepped outside of the Mammy Felleh Cookery Shop, a jubilant scene greeted me. Taxi drivers had little flags on the sides of their bonnets bearing the colors and logos of the teams they supported. They blasted their car horns. The radio station was running a pre-analysis of the match. The streets were rife with arguments. "Let the match begin!"

"I am thirsty for professional football. Let it play!"

"Bet my watch in favor of the Eagles!" one bystander offered to another, unstrapping his gold watch.

"I bet my best watch for Lions!" another unstrapped his silver colored watch.

"First goal by the Eagles, I bet my gold chain!"

"First goal by Lions, I bet chain for chain!"

Gig, approved the match! How was he able to get the Eagles to hit the road, a road we knew the president had commanded barricaded to frustrate a rebel attack into Freetown? I turned the question over repeatedly in my mind.

On the high street, expectant people had lined the streets stretching up to a mile. The sun had gone down for a drink, where the Rokel stitched with the Atlantic Ocean. Nobody expected it would suddenly return in the sky. Quenched, it would just go to bed. The police had tried to disperse the crowd, but they had failed. They now busied themselves with diverting traffic while men and women sat in them, gulping beers. Children grouped in teams and played backyard football with larger than life names coming to their lips.

"Pass it to me, Pele!"

"Ball here, Maradona!"

"Kick it to me, Roger Miller."

I dismissed them after I realized they were grouping into backyard teams a whole history of world football, of stars born in different countries and in different generations. Dogs, the mangy and the rabid, barked at passers-by in a torment known only to them. I raised my eyes to the outskirts of the city and saw the hills crouched in dark muteness. Perhaps, only the dogs knew at that moment that the land was still at war.

I saw the two big fellows leading a mammoth crowd of celebrants on Kissy Road. They arrived at the Upgun Junction where many years ago, the British had mounted their cannons to repel a possible French invasion from neighboring Guinea into colonial Freetown.

The crowd was divided into two factions that fell into a long line on either side of the road. Choruses rang out long and loud. The waiting had been long, but the crowd's expectation hadn't been daunted. Before it sank into the ocean, the last ray of the sun had blazed as though lulled by the choruses.

A little later, the black dust of night hung in the insalubrious air. The peeping eyes of hurricane lamps were awakened on the edges of street stalls. Occasionally, bright beams of distant headlights glowed before they disappeared off a bend. The crowd continued to endure. In the dark, there were faint ebleaguered hopes.

"They will come," said one man in the crowd. "They are on their way. They don't have to play until tomorrow evening, so they have all the time they need to arrive tonight. They will surely arrive in Freetown tonight."

"My Eagles will come with claws ready for the grasp!" another concurred.

"Come on, Eagles, the Lions will show you what they are made of!"

"Fly, fly, and fly, Eagles of the sky, the people hunger for a game!"

"Roar, roar, and roar, Lions of the jungle, and wake up the gods from their lazy beds!"

Suddenly, a blast cut across the impenetrable darkness, whistling with ineluctable power. An abrupt silence followed. Stillness seized every breath. A second blast spat, like breaking china, shattering the air behind the hills. In the eerie silence, an eternal voice screamed,

"Dem don kam! Dem don kam!"

The crowd merged into one being, thundering with excitement. It surged to welcome the expected. Blasts ricocheted in the dark with tongues of fire descending on the crowd. Multiple languages cracked from within and the union of one suddenly fragmented. The moments suddenly turned cruel. Yet, the large mass at the rear pressed forward, as a new language of despair emerged from crushed bones ahead.

The rebels had entered Freetown!

Flashes continued to cut into the darkness, spilling over houses, setting them on fire. The remnants of the crowd gave way, and the rebels merged with them. Excitement turned into fear. Cheering turned into wailing. Suddenly death was coiling on everyone's doorstep.

As vigilantes, we were late to respond, but it wasn't hard for us to regroup, since most of us were already together around at the bonfires. Without waiting for a command, we spilled over, poised for action. We didn't have to close in on the rebels; the national army was already on the defensive. The soldiers asked us to comb our neighborhoods for snipers. We felt emasculated by the request until three vigilantes were gunned down from unsuspected windows. Then we became nervous.

A hand pulled me from behind, and I farted in the darkness. I knew I couldn't turn around quickly enough to shoot my attacker, so I sprawled on the ground. The figure slowly came upon me.

"*Shhhhh*," Mrs. Gimi More said.

"Badamaci, I have been searching for you everywhere," she said.

"Don't you see we have been attacked?" The smell of rancid sex and anger came to my nose.

"I know, I know, but—I have to…it's my husband," she was breathing heavily.

"What about your husband?" I thundered.

"Gig has found out about you and me. And he is mad," she began to cry.

At once I wanted to tell her it was her funeral. But then the thought of Gig's story cut across my mind, and I realized why a female corpse was not necessarily a dead woman. His wife, Mrs. Gimi More, had become a corpse to him. Gig had learned about my affair with his wife before the night he told me the story. *So, the story he had told me was about my undoing; I was the young man who had discovered his wife as the African Nomoli. I was the young man who would be the urgent revolutionary to go to war and never to be heard from again. That's why Gig had said that the war had taken a lot from his wife.*

"What did he say? How did he know about our affair?" I made a show of doubting her statement.

"Oh, Badamaci, Gig knows everything about you and me in the bedroom. Up to and including the number of times we have had sex. He talked with hate about the roughness and stench of the bedcovers," she burst out crying anew.

I could smell the covers, too. The sweat running down our joints, the small *Mm* towel we had used to wipe our properties wet with semen. I could hear the noisy love-making on the hard hunch of the bed and feel again our moments of collapse. For the first time I learned why a man would kill for his wife. Mrs. Gimi More cried harder, probably only then confronting the reality of cheating.

"It will be okay," I told her.

She cried harder. At the same time, the gunfire grew closer. She didn't even seem to be aware of it.

"You have to leave this place now," I said. "It is dangerous for you to be here. You don't want to get shot."

"What about yourself? Let us get away from here."

"I have a task. You have to go at once," I said, merely to get her away from me.

"But I am afraid Gig will hurt me. And I also have something else to tell you."

"And what would that be?"

She hesitated and looked deeply into my eyes. "I want to know whether, you really do love me."

I felt a burning anger at her foolishness. "You know very well that I do," I lied.

"I don't know that you do, but I'll be satisfied with that."

After a short pause, she took my hand into hers. "Badamaci, can we run away from here?"

"Run away? What do you mean?"

"I have Gig's money with me. I have buried it somewhere. We can go to England or to America."

"You have to think about visas," I said muttering the first thing that came to my mind.

"Our money can buy them. With money, you can buy any visa."

"How much money do you think you need?" I tried not to exhibit excitement.

"What can't we have with ten million Leones?"

I tried converting the Leones into dollars, since the Leones had lost considerable value. "Don't tell me that is what you have!"

"That's what Gig handed to me yesterday. I didn't count it, but he told me that's what was in the bag. Wait, he said he had stones in it, but I don't know what they are for."

"Where is the bag?"

"I have buried it somewhere."

"You know—please, first let us save your life. We shall talk when this battle is contained."

After a while I was able to convince her to seek refuge at the Mammy Felleh Cookery Shop, where I promised to meet her later. I knew I was supposed to be a combatant in this battle, but later in the dark, I stole away from the action. There were, in fact, too many child-combatants with rifles running all over the place.

The night pumped hot air into me. I hesitated for a moment, surveying the chaos around me. Mrs. Gimi More ran on ahead. In fear that she might get too far ahead of me, I began to move toward the Mammy Felleh Cookery Shop again. Then, suddenly, the world (or my world) stood still. I heard Gig calling me from behind. I couldn't make him out in the dark, for he held a brilliant torch toward me. It took a while for me to realize that when he called out, *"friidg,"* he meant that I should stay still (or freeze!) He began to move towards me.

"You could get killed for being careless," he said.

There was calmness in his voice, but it was pregnant with rage.

"Why are you stealing away from action? You wanted to be an officer in the army, and I trusted you. Do you enjoy being a thief? Running away from action is molestation to the quick and the dead. Didn't you learn that in the University? If you were a child of God, you would know why Christ took those nails. However, you are too sectarian to be able to understand why a man doesn't fornicate with war. You are a disgrace to your country. How many times have I asked you to provide leadership? Of course, without morals there can be no leadership."

I boiled within.

"Gig is mad," I recalled Mrs. Gimi More saying to me. I began to defend myself. "I didn't do…"

"I have not asked you!" he shouted. "*Sheeet!*" I heard the long drag of his American slang. The dim figure behind the bright hot torch seemed to be searching for something on his body.

"Where did I put it?"

I knew at once that he had left his gun somewhere, and that he confronted me with only his mug, filled with black coffee. I also knew that he intended to shoot me in cold blood. I suddenly remembered every act of brutality taught to me at the University: Hitler gassing the Jews in Germany, the creative genocide meted out to Fyodor Dostoevsky's peasants in Russia, the slaughterhouse of Idi Amin in Uganda, America condemning its Black souls to lynching, the British efforts at wiping the Aborigines from the face of the earth in Australia. It dawned on me that killing others is not so much about hating them as it is about self-preservation. You could even say, "May your soul rest in perfect peace," before disfiguring someone. I did just that. I cocked my gun, shut my eyes, and squeezed the trigger. When I opened my eyes, I saw his torch on the ground. I took it and turned its dancing light onto a motionless Gig.

Yellow flames loomed from housetops, licking with the thirst of the dry throats of the beasts of hell. I, once again, made my way toward the Mammy Felleh Cookery Shop. Nothing prepared me for the destruction there. Bundles of zinc were melted to the ground as dying flints sprang wildly about. I pointed the torch over the bodies sprawling around. Among them I found Mammy Felleh, the two big fellows, and my University colleague, who ate his lunch at the expensive Gem restaurant. My University colleague died wearing his waistcoat, with his necktie twisted behind his back. What was he doing at Mammy Felleh's? Someone was limping ahead. I flashed the light in that direction, but was unable to see who it was. Just then, the figure stopped.

"Shoot me, Gig! Kill me! I am the only one standing alive that knows you are a rebel spy. You will perish in hell for the people killed because of your soccer-scam-trap. You will roast in hell, rebel!"

The laconic voice went silent for a while as its owner continued limping away. The dim figure looked back over its shoulder again. The voice came very much like an echo this time.

"And you know what will happen? Badamaci will make love to your woman in the mouth on top of your grave!"

I thrust Gig's torch forward and saw the frail man moving away down the road.

I followed him. Occasionally, he disappeared around a bend in the road. However, because he limped, I was soon able to close the gap between us. He did not look back again, even though the firing continued behind us both. Though I was still baffled about the connection between Gig and the frail man, I recalled all that had happened in the day. Innocent and useful lives like that of Mammy Felleh that had been lost. I also wondered what could have happened to the soccer team from Kono. Then, I recalled the argument at the cookery shop. I remembered the two big fellows had agreed that the Eagles team was indeed a good team. No wonder tickets were sold out before noon. And now, here was the frail man talking about my relationship with Gig's wife. I still couldn't connect it all.

The frail man collapsed in the dark but quickly picked himself up again. I noticed he was dragging his left leg and struggled to pull it along with his left hand. When I saw his condition, I hurried to close the remaining distance between us. Soon, I nearly ran into him. I was close enough to touch him before I realized that he had stopped walking. He turned around to look at me. I flashed the torch on his face.

"No, no, Gig, you are not going to kill me because you need the stones. You can't have them from a dead man," he collapsed on the road again.

"What are you talking about, Socrates?" I shouted.

"Who is this?" he sat up.

"My name is Badamaci."

He touched my hand and said, "I know you. His torch, Gig's torch, how did you get it?"

I did not answer. I led him to the side of the road and helped him sit on a rock. He breathed heavily, but his strength seemed to be returning to him. He winced when he tried to move his left leg. He groaned and cussed. He asked me to hold the torch near his wound. A bullet had ripped his flesh, leaving a jagged tear. His blood ran all the way to his toes.

"Gig is trying to kill me," he said.

He told me that he and Gig had grown up together in the same house, which the frail man called a family house. Socrates may not have been a successful carpenter by urban standards, but he and his family were able to live hand-to-mouth in their small village. A year ago, Gig began to send urgent messages for him to visit him in Freetown.

"The city had frustrated me before, so I had shied away from it," he said.

But Gig had bombarded him with many promises. With the urging of the elders in the village, he had left his wife and children behind and had come to visit Gig. Gig was no longer the humble dock worker Socrates had known. He now drove big cars and wore tinted glasses.

"We were all afraid for his lifestyle," Socrates said. "We thought that he was going too deep into corruption, a state of affairs we feared he did not properly understand."

Quiet for a while, Socrates turned to me and said, "Sit down Badamaci, sit down. I have more things to tell you."

I sat on a rock close to him.

Gig had told the frail man he wanted to make him a detective. There were suddenly too many enemies around him. He would be vulnerable to them if he didn't find an extra pair of eyes to watch his back. The frail man was led into a secret only because he was a true brother. Gig had reminded him of the blood bond between them and of the family spirit in both. The frail man understood the blood, the spirit, and the ties. He added to them the honor of being asked to benefit from a brother's opportunities.

"Two men are on my trail," Gig had told him.

"Did you say two men are on your trail? What for?" the frail man had asked Gig.

"We are in a war over our heads. You are aware of that, aren't you?"

"But why are two men on *your* trail?" the frail man had pushed. "That's too personal."

"That's true, that's true," Gig agreed. "That's why you are here…do you hold your vows of the Poro Society sacred?"

"I hold them sacred, you know that," the frail man had answered, not knowing where the conversation was leading.

"Swear you'll be a man and not a woman in the face of adversity. That you'll die if you reveal."

"Reveal? Reveal what? Where is this going?" Socrates had protested.

"Does a messenger tell a message before or after greeting?"

"It has to be after greeting."

"Well?" Gig asked, having made his point.

The frail man had sworn.

That was why Socrates had been on the trail of the two big fellows. He had secretly followed them wherever they went, listened to what they said, to whom they talked, and, if possible, what they thought. At this point I recalled the argument he'd had with the two big fellows at Mammy Felleh Cookery Shop. Gig had considered the two big fellows dangerous. He wanted twenty-four-hour surveillance on them. He provided the frail man with a mobile cell phone that he was to use to call him if anything came up. However, an incident which happened on one day made the frail man almost keel over. He had walked into Gig's office and found him and the two big fellows chatting over coffee and beer. When he got over his shock, and after the two big fellows had left, the frail man had told Gig that it was no longer necessary to trail the big fellows.

"Why do you say that? Don't you understand? You have to keep your eyes on them until…"

"Until what, Gig? Are they not considered friends?"

"Look here, Socrates. Sit down! I guess I have to make you understand this business better. You see, there is something going on—kind of weird—and you know it is all part of bringing the war to an end. After I became head of the vigilante movement, I received a letter from the rebel leader, that he wanted me to broker an agreement between himself and the president, so that they could end the war and form a government of national unity. There is the promise of power and stones: I mean clean diamonds! There is promise of money if I can—you know—help them, I mean the rebels, reach Freetown. And you know what that means for you and the other good people back in the village. The point is that the rebels want to negotiate from a position of strength. They figure if they are in control of half of Freetown, the government will listen to them."

"But, Gig, you know these guys. You know what they are capable of doing."

"Listen, I have been assured that there will be no trouble when they come. Only last week, I advised the president and the Association of Sierra Leone Footballers that the Eagles could be invited for the match that the president had postponed. At the same time, I have assured the rebels that they could surreptitiously come with the team if they promise to open the road on their end a month before the game and not hurt the players and their delegation," he explained.

"Back to Extro and Intro, they have been planted on me by the rebels to ensure I was making my promise real."

The frail man suddenly broke off this startling account of the conversation he'd had with Gig. Then I was able to connect the bits to form a whole. I flashed the torch at him. He was pale and weak. He still had his hand on his wound. I offered to carry him on my back, but he declined and said he wanted to talk to some more. The guns had almost all quieted except a few irritating snipers occasionally blasting in the dark. He took my hands into his. I could feel his whole body trembling like that of a very old man. He said he had a confession to make.

"Well, of course I'm not sorry for the first one," he began. "Extro and Intro are dead. They were mutilated by a civilian crowd. I did what Gig told me to do if they got out of hand. I shouted 'rebels' at them and the crowd simply went wolf-hungry." He smirked for a moment and then continued. "And it was I who told Gig about you and his wife. I had been spying on you and Mrs. More. You have to understand…I had sworn to Gig I would protect his interest and…"

"I understand," I said, patting him on the back. "You had to do what you had to do."

Just then the bush rustled. I flashed the torch in the direction of the noise. There was Gig standing as if he were Lazarus, asked to walk out of the tomb. His gun was pointed in our direction. I could see the shattered shoulder where my bullet had done its damage. He cocked his gun. He ordered me to point the torch first towards myself and then toward the frail man.

"Ah, so it's you two," he breathed. "Socrates, where are my diamonds? Hand them over to me, and I'll let yo**u go."

He asked me to point the torch toward myself again. "Mr. Traitor, I'm not sure you'll make love to another man's woman so soon. You'd have to wait until after judgment day. How would you like this right between your legs?"

My throat went dry.

I felt a tremendous jolt and a split second later, I heard the bullet explode out of Gig's weapon.

My head crashed on a rock, and I was flat on my back. The frail man rolled away from me as he thudded on the ground. He had saved my life and had been shot instead of me. I quickly reached for my gun and fired six bullets into Gig's stomach. It was the second time I'd used a gun, and both times I'd used it on the same person. He was dead before he reached the ground. I turned to Socrates and cupped his head in my palms.

"You are going to be okay, Socrates. I'm going to take you to an emergency unit."

"It doesn't matter anymore, Badamaci. I just have to tell you one more thing, before I—before—I…"

I interrupted him. I knew what he was trying to say. "You are going to be fine," I said.

"You ought to be thanking your stars, Badamaci," he said.

"Yeah, but why is that?"

"The two big fellows were supposed to kill you just after the rebels stormed Freetown. I saw them threatening Mrs. More to tell them where you were." Just then he gasped, and spat his life into my hands.

I thought about the diamonds somewhere whose whereabouts were forever locked in the head of the corpse of the frail man. Soon, I remembered that Mrs. Gimi More knew something about them. I recalled the plans she had for the two of us. I picked up the torch and began to retrace my way to Mammy Felleh Cookery shop.

I looked among the corpses, but I didn't find her. As I began to leave the scene, I heard her familiar cry under a fallen tree. I dashed toward the painful sound, and there she was. I urged her to approach as I raised the torch, but under the tree, couched in the agony of double mutilation, she lay sprawled with the blood of rape all over her. And beside her, were the shattered pieces of her husband's coffee mug with its reflection like a mirror looking without a memory.

THE DEVIL IN THE MAIL

Since his arrival in America, Bantha had twice visited a bar, but there was no one to talk to, as there was no one he knew. The only thing that kept him sitting for three beers in a row was the music and the banter around him. He conquered his loneliness by eavesdropping on any conversation his ears could catch. Eventually he was always left lonelier than when he'd arrived. The only other thing that brought fire to his heart was his mail, which regularly brought him fines in America or messages from Africa. Like tomorrow, he would be scheduled to attend a small claims court.

The morning, before attending court, he collected the previous day's mail from his home post, but he had no time to read the letters. He stacked them on the front passenger seat, and there they remained cold and mute, but not without a life in them. As if he heard them rustling in their envelopes, he began to pick them one after the other, but only to read the envelopes and throw them into the car's back seat.

As it flung open into Maryland's frosty morning weather, Bantha Bangura ran out the giant aluminum door. His hands were in gloves before he left the Traffic Offences Law Court. He sat in his car motionless for a brief while and suddenly felt warm tears trickling down his cheeks. He removed his gloves and blew warm air onto his cold and hardened fingers, his wintry breath spiraling and puffing toward the windscreen.

At first, his traffic court appearances didn't bother him, but the hours he had to attend were taking a toll on his pay cheque. Another major effect was that he could no longer keep his promise to send monthly support to Africa, to his extended family, who, had dedicatedly, continued to increase their letters of reminder to him.

There were more fines and charges of reckless driving in his post; most of the charges, he noticed, registered the hours he was running from one job to the other. He then saw the usual flow of letters from his relatives in the African country of Kaibara, requesting his urgent intervention in matters of school fees, funeral ceremonies, and ceremonies of traditional rites of passage for young girls in the village; attempts at establishing businesses, and requests to build houses for uncles and aunts.

Just as he was getting fed up with all the mails, one envelope caught his eyes. His heart missed a beat. What was the letter about and from whom? He keenly looked at it a second time, but the envelope gave no clue. He hoped it was not any matter his family had with the law to which he was being drawn.

His father had always taught him obeisance for the law. It was for this reason, in fact, that when he announced that he had gotten a visa to migrate to America, his father was excited that his son had been rescued from the pettiness of politicians, who were always ready to milk the young and vulnerable and dump them by the proverbial way side at the mercy of the fowls of the air. He had been the first person in his family to have ever crossed over the Atlantic Ocean for greener pastures.

He tore the envelope and a long letter issued out. The letter reported that a Kaibara court summons had been served to two members of his family because they knowingly gave the hand of a minor, aged twelve, in marriage to a newly retired government worker who had relocated to the village to resettle.

"Dad, uncles, aunts, brothers and sisters," Bantha had told his family on his last night before leaving the African soil for America, "I admonish you all to stop giving your young girls in marriage to older men; in fact, to anyone whomsoever, when such girls should be going to school."

They had all assured him that such a practice would stop as from that day. Only six months later the feared crime threatened to incinerate his family. Brooding over his checkered life in America, since his migration, and the challenges of ethics and of poverty haunting his family at home, he ignited the car's engine and hit the road. That morning Goodluck Road, messy with snow, caused his car to swerve. He suddenly felt like jumping off the world, or finding a small corner outside of it, to be alone to himself; not in his car, not even in his one room apartment.

Everywhere and every situation had become claustrophobia to his life. He gunned the car down a left road, leading to his apartment. Without realizing it, he ran through a red light. He felt the camera flashing twice in his face. It was too late! He instantly spewed a *shit* expression! Another ticket would be on its way to him soon, he knew.

Why was Tamba, his father, allowing everything to slip away from his hands in Kaibara? Was he not the man who had brought Bantha up to a mind of chain and steel? Bantha didn't remember any moment he and his father had spoken about the envious position of the father, being the first man in the family whose child had gone abroad, a situation that automatically catapulted the father to the position of guardian of the family clan, bridging the dynasty between the living and the dead members of the family?

According to Bantha, Tamba was supposed to speak up and speak truth in honor of change! He should have seen that not one member of the family strayed away or did anything that distracted the attention of his son abroad from fending for members of the family. And now the scandal of a few members of the family threatened to incinerate the entire clan. But to think that, Tamba, the poor father of twenty-five children, now seriously hit hard by time and condition, an aged rock, was wasting away?

Sitting closer to his letter pouch, Bantha retrieved the most recent summons of his speeding offense. Opening the summons to where it read *The State of Maryland vs. Bantha Bangura,* he shouted, *yes!* The mischievous thought that had startled him suddenly tickled him with laughter. He built up a gradual breath of giggling before discharging a loud outburst of uncontrollable laughter. As he sank in his bed, he felt his lungs hurting from his wild laugh. He knew he had to send a mail to his father, as planned that moment.

***

The frustration in Tamba Bangura as he cooled himself from the African heat showed prominently in his face. He rested on a rock shaded by a giant tree in a field beside a bush path. His shoulders stooped with the fear that thousands of miles away from him, his son, Bantha, was suffering under the terror of the white man, all because of the greed of the family at home, who kept pushing the young man to give them everything American. And there Bantha was, sued in court, by the government of an entire state in that philistine country.

How scandalous!

Tamba held a copy of the Maryland Traffic Offences Law Court summons that had been served Bantha Bangura, close to his palpitating heart. A week earlier, Bantha had mailed it to his father in Kaibara, hoping the summons would generate sympathy for him and stave off any more requests for help from any member of the family, at least in the immediate period. Tamba had only shared its contents with his two other brothers whom he had cautioned to keep sealed lips over the matter while they decided what to do. However, a thought kept twisting a question in his mind: what could he really do about a matter he could not comprehend and that was happening thousands of miles away from him? Since receiving the mail from his son about the whole disconcerting matter of *The State of Maryland vs. Bantha Bangura,* Tamba couldn't sleep well at night?

Who would be able to fight against a state? Bantha had once told his father on the phone that Maryland was bigger and more

106

populous than was Kaibara. And on top of that, what power did a stranger have over a generous-turned-angry host? Tamba remembered that his son had once mentioned to him the number of African immigrants in American jails. Was his son heading for such an end after a journey to America that had cost Tamba almost everything he ever had?

Something had to be done!

Something, anything to protect the life of his son and to avert the scandal awaiting—it was that resolve that caused him to wait along the road for his brothers' arrival, at that rock, in the open field beside the bush path, so that they could execute the plan they had agreed on.

The brothers arrived, and the journey took off and ended at a soothsayer's shrine seven forests away from their town. The soothsayer requested from the brothers three white lambs representing the love of the three brothers for the son of Tamba. They submitted the three white lambs. He requested three of their own individual blood in drained test tubes. They submitted them.

Even after several incantations, the matter remained dark to the soothsayer's inner eye. Bantha told them that it was because the matter was far away across the ocean.

The soothsayer requested a bit of the daylight sun and the three brothers eyed each other hopelessly. The soothsayer knew it was an impossible request, especially made at night, and he explained to them that he had no power over the requests that came to his lips. He explained to them that every genuine soothsayer was only a messenger and that thirty candles would do to burn like the rays of the sun.

They quickly provided those.

After sweating profusely in his shrine, the soothsayer suddenly caught a glimpse of the white man's city on the other side beside the great ocean, in his mirror. The mirror creaked.

"Images are emerging from the edges of the ocean over on the other side." The soothsayer uttered a brief incantation before continuing: "The matter of your son in America is now crystal clear. But I see too many difficulties strewn to it." He paced his shrine, back and forth, uttering more incantations. "The white man is determined to twist the matter from right to left until water is squeezed out where it never was."

Tamba gasped and squealed. He felt the pain of the soothsayer's words in his belly. His two brothers soothed him.

"Money," the soothsayer noted, "has to exchange hands before the matter could die."

The mirror was blind again. The soothsayer laid it aside. The candles had all almost burned out.

The two brothers on each side of Tamba rose from where they sat, but Tamba remained nailed down to his seat, pinned by the gloomy memory of his severe relationship with Bantha, when the latter was only a boy. He regretted not encouraging his son when he was a child; instead, he'd spanked him mercilessly anytime a complaint was made against him. He felt that between father and son a time of grass had burnt, perishable of hope, for both. And now a whole state, on a foreign continent, had clawed his boy's bones by the shoulders, and was leading him through a garrison, to the gallows.

Lost in thought, he felt the cold soft hands of one of his brothers on him, urging him to rise and walk. The incantation picked up his lanky body and made him walk ahead of his brothers. The other brother reached to his inner dwindling courage, offering recitations of Quaranic verses to soothe his soul.

Tamba clenched a fist and kept walking like Lazarus from the dead.

***

For a month after Bantha mailed his father a copy of the Maryland court summons against him, as a way of scaring the family from making unreasonable demands of him, Bantha did not receive a single mail from Kaibara. He erupted with laughter each time he opened his mail box and did not see any mail from his native land.

One day, he saw an unusually blue envelope in his mailbox. Quickly picking it up, he suspected it to have come from Kaibara. All the other pieces of he held in his hands fell to the floor. Still looking at the envelope, he walked to a nearby chair and sank into it, clearly examining every detail of the envelope. He tore it open and withdrew a wad of papers from it.

He leaned against the chair as he continued to study the papers in his hands. There was a long letter spanning three pages of calligraphic print. He began to read through a few lines, but anxiety got the whole of him, and he instead simply browsed through the pages, wondering what had caused his father to dictate such copious notes to him. Suddenly feeling thirsty, he placed the papers on the table and went to the kitchen for a pint of beer.

Taking a long sip, he breathed heavily and felt the anxiety diminishing in his system. He took two more sips and threw the pint in his trashcan and returned to his chair, more determined to read the letter.

"But for the ocean between us, my son, I could have borne your pain!" Tamba had dictated in the letter.

Tamba explained that he had returned from the soothsayer direct to his village where he had gathered a large family meeting to break the egg of secrecy. The family had met to discuss *The State of Maryland vs. Bantha Bangura* court summons. When the title summons was read at the meeting, many could not believe their ears. How could a whole government go after one man, their son, in a marathon of court order? The men were bereaved, and the women were bereaved.

Members of the family couldn't hold back their tears.

After the news had been reported, the entire compound wailed. Women and children rolled on the ground as though they had received news of bereavement.

"Is this not bereavement or worse than?" Tamba, reduced to tears, had exclaimed. "When one has palaver with an entire country, where in God's kingdom does one hide?"

The mothers in the family broke into a song of mourning:

But for the ocean between us,
We would have come over to mourn with you.
The waters that separate us
Do not measure the depth of our tears.
O seas, carry our tears to the ocean.
O ocean, carry our tears to our son!

Suddenly a piece of paper fell from the blue envelope. It was a MoneyGram invoice in the amount of $5,000 sent to Bantha to help him pay his court cost, in the matter between him and the state of Maryland.

Bantha couldn't believe his eyes. He pinched himself. How could they do such a thing? His prank had only meant...only meant...only meant...

"Oh my, O, dear God!" He lamented.

Restless, Bantha grabbed his car keys, draped his shirt over his shoulders and disappeared out the front door. In less than an hour, he was standing before a clerk at MoneyGram receiving the money his father had sent.

His mind raced back to the letter, and how his father had narrated where the money he sent him had come from: the village had done a combined rice harvest, school children had staged skits and dramas and had raised a few amount of money toward the targeted amount, every widow had raised a fist of her might and had dropped her coin in, too.

So, Bantha thought, if an African family could raise an amount that huge in such a short time, all that his people ever needed to do was to resolve to find local solutions to their challenges and not to sit and wait for foreign donors…who would require them to mortgage an identity for funding.

The clerk shifted the bundle of $500 notes to him at the window and asked him to sign. He signed the papers, but stopped short of receiving the money. The clerk assured him it was all his.

He cleared his throat and said to the clerk that the money was no longer his, and that it was on its way back to Kaibara.

The clerk tightened her face in disbelief before agreeing to begin the process of returning the money to Kaibara. In ten minutes, the process was done and the money began its journey back to Bantha's native land.

"Dad," Bantha said on the phone when he returned to his apartment, "Thank you and all of my family members for the letter of comfort and the money you sent me."

"Bantha, are you alright?" Tamba screamed on the phone. "We are putting together a work force to raise more money…"

"Dad, Dad, Dad!"

His father went silent.

"There is no need to raise any more money for me. The court case between the State of Maryland and I, is over; the matter was thrown out of court because the policeman who pulled me over for speeding failed to show up in court."

The line remained silent.

"Dad!"

Tamba cleared his throat. "I'm not sure of what you are talking about. Your neck is about to be wrung by the white man's government, and you are telling me because a policeman didn't show up in court the matter is finished? Meaning you won the case?"

"It's over, Dad. It's over."

In a high pitch of tone, and away from his phone, Tamba spoke, as if from a distance, "My son has won an entire court case between him and a state in America! Yet, in Kaibara, a country smaller than that state, many lawyers put together, cannot ever win a case against a village."

Bantha heard a vociferous applause at the background.

"This calls for celebration!" a voice thundered.

Another voice cried, "Bring us a jug of palm wine from the tapper."

"What a sweet palm oil of words are pouring from your lips, my brothers. And now a true son of Kaibara has humbled an entire state of a country in the White man's land. Drink to this feat of great deed. The white man shall not forget about this defeat in a hurry."

Bantha breathed a heavy sigh into his cell phone and when his father returned, with his attention, he said, "Dad, listen to me, I didn't…"

"I know you didn't do anything wrong that's why you won the case!"

"Dad, let's just say that the State dropped the matter against me," Bantha wanted the matter concluded between the two of them.

"Yes, I can understand my son," his dad emphasized. "The soothsayer mentioned how much the State wanted to squeeze you dry, and now you have won the matter, and, *left with no choice*, the state decided to drop the matter."

After a brief silence, in which Bantha allowed the euphoria on the other side to subside, the father spoke again and burst into a loud and longer laughter.

"Dad, I've sent the money back to Freetown."

"What are we going to do with it?"

"I want you and the other elders in the family to open an account, give it any name, and begin a trust fund for the children of our village, especially girls. Lead a campaign against marrying off young girls away and prioritize their learning. If we do that, dad, in no time, our village will be full of educated young men and women. And that's what we need for our development."

"I agree with you, son, I agree."

"Dad, I have ordered my bank to transfer the sum of $500 more as my support to your noble venture."

Tamba again spoke away from his mouth piece, "Bantha didn't even have to use the money we sent him!" He shouted. "He won the case without a penny from his pocket! He has even returned us the $500 we sent him."

Silence!